ERICH SEGAL

Love Story

hachette
INDIA

First published in the United States of America by Harper and Row in 1970
First published in Great Britain by Hodder & Stoughton in 1970
This edition published in 2006 by Hodder & Stoughton
A division of Hodder Headline

A Hodder paperback

11

A CIP catalogue record for this title is
available from the British Library

ISBN 978-1- 4447-7696-6

Typeset in Sabon LT Std by Eleven Arts, New Delhi

Printed and bound in India by Manipal Technologies Ltd, Manipal

Hodder Headline's policy is to use papers that are natural, renewable
and recyclable products and made from wood grown in sustainable forests.
The logging and manufacturing processes are expected to conform to
the environmental regulations of the country of origin.

Hodder & Stoughton Ltd
A division of Hodder Headline
338 Euston Road
London NW1 3BH

For Sylvia Herscher and John Flaxman

...namque ... solebatis
Meas esse aliquid putare nugas

Love Story

I

What can you say about a twenty-five-year-old girl who died?

That she was beautiful. And brilliant. That she loved Mozart and Bach. And the Beatles. And me. Once, when she specifically lumped me with those musical types, I asked her what the order was, and she replied, smiling, 'Alphabetical.' At the time I smiled too. But now I sit and wonder whether she was listing me by my first name—in which case I would trail Mozart—or by my last name—in which case I would edge in there between Bach and the Beatles. Either way I don't come first, which for some stupid reason bothers hell out of me, having grown up with the notion that I always had to be number one. Family heritage, don't you know?

* * *

In the fall of my senior year, I got into the habit of studying at the Radcliffe library. Not just to eye the cheese, although I admit that I liked to look. The place was quiet, nobody knew me, and the reserve books were less in demand. The day before one of my history hour exams, I still hadn't gotten around to reading the first book on the list, an endemic Harvard disease. I ambled over to the reserve desk to get one of the tomes that would bail me out on the morrow. There were two girls working there: one a tall tennis-anyone type, the other a bespectacled mouse type. I opted for Minnie Four-Eyes.

'Do you have *The Waning of the Middle Ages*?'

She shot a glance up at me.

'Do you have your own library?' she asked.

'Listen, Harvard is allowed to use the Radcliffe library.'

'I'm not talking legality, Preppie, I'm talking ethics. You guys have five million books. We have a few lousy thousand.'

Christ, a superior-being type! The kind who think since the ratio of Radcliffe to Harvard is five to one, the girls must be five times as smart. I normally cut these types to ribbons, but just then I badly needed that goddamn book.

'Listen, I need that goddamn book.'

'Wouldja please watch your profanity, Preppie?'

'What makes you so sure I went to prep school?'

'You look stupid and rich,' she said, removing her glasses.

'You're wrong,' I protested. 'I'm actually smart and poor.'

'Oh, no, Preppie. *I'm* smart and poor.'

She was staring straight at me. Her eyes were brown. Okay, maybe I look rich, but I wouldn't let some 'Cliffie—even one with pretty eyes—call me dumb.

'What the hell makes you so smart?' I asked.

'I wouldn't go for coffee with you,' she answered.

'Listen—I wouldn't ask you.'

'That,' she replied, 'is what makes you stupid.'

Let me explain why I took her for coffee. By shrewdly capitulating at the crucial moment—i.e. by pretending that I suddenly wanted to—I got my book. And since she couldn't leave until the library closed, I had plenty of time to absorb some pithy phrases about the shift of royal dependence from cleric to lawyer in the late eleventh century. I got an A minus on the exam, coincidentally the same grade I assigned to Jenny's legs when she first walked from behind that desk. I can't say I gave her costume an honor grade, however; it was a bit too Boho for my taste. I especially loathed that Indian thing she carried for a handbag. Fortunately I didn't mention this, as I later discovered it was of her own design.

We went to the Midget Restaurant, a nearby sandwich joint which, despite its name, is not restricted to people of small stature. I ordered two coffees and a brownie with ice cream (for her).

'I'm Jennifer Cavilleri,' she said, 'an American of Italian descent.'

As if I wouldn't have known.

'And a music major,' she added.

'My name is Oliver,' I said.

'First or last?' she asked.

'First,' I answered, and then confessed that my entire name was Oliver Barrett. (I mean that's most of it.)

'Oh,' she said. 'Barrett, like the poet?'

'Yes,' I said. 'No relation.'

In the pause that ensued, I gave inward thanks that she hadn't come up with the usual distressing question: 'Barrett, like the hall?' For it is my special albatross to be related to the guy that built Barrett Hall, the largest and ugliest structure in Harvard Yard, a colossal monument to my family's money, vanity and flagrant Harvardism.

After that, she was pretty quiet. Could we have run out of conversation so quickly?

Had I turned her off by not being related to the poet? What? She simply sat there, semi-smiling at me. For something to do, I checked out her notebooks. Her handwriting was curious—small sharp little letters with no capitals (who did she think she was, e. e. cummings?). And she was taking some pretty snowy courses: Comp. Lit. 105, Music 150, Music 201—

'Music 201? Isn't that a graduate course?'

She nodded yes, and was not very good at masking her pride.

'Renaissance polyphony.'

'What's polyphony?'

'Nothing sexual, Preppie.'

Why was I putting up with this? Doesn't she read the *Crimson*? Doesn't she know who I am?

'Hey, don't you know who I am?'

'Yeah,' she answered with kind of disdain. 'You're the guy that owns Barrett Hall.'

She didn't know who I was.

'I don't *own* Barrett Hall,' I quibbled. 'My great-grandfather happened to give it to Harvard.'

'So his not-so-great grandson would be sure to get in!'

That was the limit.

'Jenny, if you're so convinced I'm a loser, why did you bulldoze me into buying you coffee?'

She looked me straight in the eye and smiled.

'I like your body,' she said. Part of being a big winner is the ability to be a good loser. There's no paradox involved. It's a distinctly Harvard thing to be able to turn any defeat into victory.

'*Tough luck, Barrett. You played a helluva game.*'

'*Really, I'm so glad you fellows took it. I mean, you people need to win so badly.*'

Of course, an out-and-out triumph is better. I mean, if you have the option, the last-minute score is preferable. And as I walked Jenny back to her dorm, I had not despaired of ultimate victory over this snotty Radcliffe bitch.

'Listen, you snotty Radcliffe bitch, Friday night is the Dartmouth hockey game.'

'So?'

'So I'd like you to come.'

She replied with the usual Radcliffe reverence for sport:

'Why the hell should I come to a lousy hockey game?'

I answered casually:

'Because I'm playing.'

There was a brief silence. I think I heard snow falling.

'For which side?' she asked.

II

Oliver Barrett IV   *Senior*
Ipswich, Mass.   *Phillips Exeter*
Age 20   *5' 11", 185 lbs.*
Major: Social Studies
Dean's List: '61, '62, '63
All-Ivy First Team: '62, '63
Career Aim: Law

By now Jenny had read my bio in the program. I made triple sure that Vic Claman, the manager, saw that she got one.

'For *Christ's* sake, Barrett, is this your first date?'

'*Shut up, Vic, or you'll be chewing your teeth.*'

As we warmed up on the ice, I didn't wave to her (how uncool!) or even look her way. And yet I think she *thought* I was glancing at her. I mean, did she remove her glasses during the National Anthem out of respect for the flag?

By the middle of the second period, we were beating Dartmouth 0–0. That is, Davey Johnston and I were about to perforate their nets. The Green bastards sensed this, and began to play rougher. Maybe they could break a bone or two before we broke them open. The fans were already screaming for blood. And in hockey this literally means blood or, failing that, a goal. As a kind of noblesse oblige, I have never denied them either.

Al Redding, Dartmouth center, charged across our blue line and I slammed into him, stole the puck and started down-ice. The fans were roaring. I could see Davey Johnston on my left, but I thought I would take it all the way, their goalie being a slightly chicken type I had terrorized since he played for Deerfield. Before I could get off a shot, both their defensemen were on me, and I had to skate around their nets to keep hold of the puck. There were three of us, flailing away against the boards and each other. It had always been my policy, in pile-ups like this, to lash mightily at anything wearing enemy colors. Somewhere beneath our skates was the puck, but for the moment we were concentrating on beating the shit out of each other.

A ref blew his whistle.

'You—two minutes in the box!'

I looked up. He was pointing at me. Me? What had I done to deserve a penalty?

'Come on, ref, what'd I do?'

Somehow he wasn't interested in further

dialogue. He was calling to the officials' desk—'Number seven, two minutes'—and signaling with his arms.

I remonstrated a bit, but that's de rigueur. The crowd expects a protest, no matter how flagrant the offense. The ref waved me off. Seething with frustration, I skated toward the penalty box. As I climbed in, listening to the click of my skate blades on the wood of the floor, I heard the bark of the PA system:

'Penalty. Barrett of Harvard. Two minutes. Holding.'

The crowd booed; several Harvards impugned the vision and integrity of the referees. I sat, trying to catch my breath, not looking up or even out onto the ice, where Dartmouth outmanned us.

'Why are you sitting here when all your friends are out playing?'

The voice was Jenny's. I ignored her, and exhorted my teammates instead.

'C'mon, Harvard, get that puck!'

'What did you do wrong?'

I turned and answered her. She was my date, after all.

'I tried too hard.'

And I went back to watching my teammates try to hold off Al Redding's determined efforts to score.

'Is this a big disgrace?'

'Jenny, please, I'm trying to concentrate!'

'On what?'

'On how I'm gonna total that bastard Al Redding!'

I looked out onto the ice to give moral support to my colleagues.

'Are you a dirty player?'

My eyes were riveted on our goal, now swarming with Green bastards. I couldn't wait to get out there again. Jenny persisted.

'Would you ever "total" me?'

I answered her without turning.

'I will right now if you don't shut up.'

'I'm leaving. Good-bye.'

By the time I turned, she had disappeared. As I stood up to look further, I was informed that my two-minute sentence was up. I leaped the barrier, back onto the ice.

The crowd welcomed my return. Barrett's on wing, all's right with the team. Wherever she was hiding, Jenny would hear the big enthusiasm for my presence. So who cares where she is.

Where is she?

Al Redding slapped a murderous shot, which our goalie deflected off toward Gene Kennaway, who then passed it down-ice in my vicinity. As I skated after the puck, I thought I had a split second to glance up at the stands to search for Jenny. I did. I saw her. She was there.

The next thing I knew I was on my ass.

Two Green bastards had slammed into me,

my ass was on the ice, and I was—Christ!—embarrassed beyond belief. Barrett dumped! I could hear the loyal Harvard fans groaning for me as I skidded. I could hear the blood-thirsty Dartmouth fans chanting.

'Hit 'em again! Hit 'em again!'

What would Jenny think?

Dartmouth had the puck around our goal again, and again our goalie deflected their shot. Kennaway pushed it at Johnston, who rifled it down to me (I had stood up by this time). Now the crowd was wild. This had to be a score. I took the puck and sped all out across Dartmouth's blue line. Two Dartmouth defensemen were coming straight at me.

'Go, Oliver, go! Knock their heads off!'

I heard Jenny's shrill scream above the crowd. It was exquisitely violent. I faked out one defenseman, slammed the other so hard he lost his breath and then—instead of shooting off balance—I passed off to Davey Johnston, who had come up the right side. Davey slapped it into the nets. Harvard score!

In an instant, we were hugging and kissing. Me and Davey Johnston and the other guys. Hugging and kissing and back slapping and jumping up and down (on skates). The crowd was screaming. And the Dartmouth guy I hit was still on his ass. The fans threw programs onto the ice. This really broke Dartmouth's back. (That's a metaphor; the defenseman got up when he caught his breath.) We creamed them 7–0.

If I were a sentimentalist, and cared enough about Harvard to hang a photograph on the wall, it would not be of Winthrop House, or Mem Church, but of Dillon. Dillon Field House. If I had a spiritual home at Harvard, this was it. Nate Pusey may revoke my diploma for saying this, but Widener Library means far less to me than Dillon. Every afternoon of my college life I walked into that place, greeted my buddies with friendly obscenities, shed the trappings of civilization and turned into a jock. How great to put on the pads and the good old number seven shirt (I had dreams of them retiring that number; they didn't), to take the skates and walk out toward the Watson Rink.

The return to Dillon would be even better. Peeling off the sweaty gear, strutting naked to the supply desk to get a towel.

'*How'd it go today, Ollie?*'

'*Good, Richie. Good, Jimmy.*'

Then into the showers to listen to who did what to whom how many times last Saturday night. '*We got these pigs from Mount Ida, see . . . ?*' And I was privileged to enjoy a private place of meditation. Being blessed with a bad knee (yes, blessed: have you seen my draft card?), I had to give it some whirlpool after playing. As I sat and watched the rings run

round my knee, I could catalog my cuts and
bruises (I enjoy them, in a way), and kind of
think about anything or nothing. Tonight I
could think of a goal, an assist and virtually
locking up my third consecutive All-Ivy.

'Takin' some whirly-pooly, Ollie?'

It was Jackie Felt, our trainer and self-
appointed spiritual guide.

'What does it look like I'm doing, Felt,
beating off?'

Jackie chortled and lit up with an idiot
grin.

'Know what's wrong with yer knee, Ollie?
Diya know?'

I'd been to every orthopedist in the East,
but Felt knew better.

'Yer not eatin' right.'

I really wasn't very interested.

'Yer not eatin' enough salt.'

Maybe if I humor him he'll go away.

'Okay, Jack, I'll start eating more salt.'

Jesus, was he pleased! He walked off with this amazing look of accomplishment on his idiot face. Anyway, I was alone again. I let my whole pleasantly aching body slide into the whirlpool, closed my eyes and just sat there, up to my neck in warmth. Ahhhhhhh.

Jesus! Jenny would be waiting outside. I hope! Still! Jesus! How long had I lingered in that comfort while she was out there in the Cambridge cold? I set a new record for getting dressed. I wasn't even quite dry as I pushed open the center door of Dillon.

The cold air hit me. God, was it freezing. And dark. There was still a small cluster of fans. Mostly old hockey faithfuls, the grads who've never mentally shed the pads. Guys like old Jordan Jencks, who come to every single game, home or away. How do they do it? I mean, Jencks is a big banker. And *why* do they do it?

'Quite a spill you took, Oliver.'

'Yeah, Mr Jencks. You know what kind of game they play.'

I was looking everywhere for Jenny. Had she left and walked all the way back to Radcliffe alone?

'Jenny?'

I took three or four steps away from the fans, searching desperately. Suddenly she popped out from behind a bush, her face swathed in a scarf, only her eyes showing.

'Hey, Preppie, it's cold as hell out here.'

Was I glad to see her!

'Jenny!'

Like instinctively, I kissed her lightly on the forehead.

'Did I say you could?' she said.

'What?'

'Did I say you could kiss me?'

'Sorry. I was carried away.'

'I wasn't.'

We were pretty much all alone out there,

and it was dark and cold and late. I kissed her again. But not on the forehead, and not lightly. It lasted a long nice time. When we stopped kissing, she was still holding on to my sleeves.

'I don't like it,' she said.

'What?'

'The fact that I like it.'

As we walked all the way back (I have a car, but she wanted to walk), Jenny held on to my sleeve. Not my arm, my sleeve. Don't ask me to explain that. At the doorstep of Briggs Hall, I did not kiss her good night.

'Listen, Jen, I may not call you for a few months.'

She was silent for a moment. A few moments.

Finally she asked, 'Why?'

'Then again, I may call you as soon as I get to my room.'

I turned and began to walk off.

'Bastard!' I heard her whisper.

I pivoted again and scored from a distance of twenty feet.

'See, Jenny, you can dish it out, but you can't take it!'

I would like to have seen the expression on her face, but strategy forbade my looking back.

My roommate, Ray Stratton, was playing poker with two football buddies as I entered the room.

'Hello, animals.'

They responded with appropriate grunts.

'Whatja get tonight, Ollie?' Ray asked.

'An assist and a goal,' I replied.

'Off Cavilleri?'

'None of your business,' I replied.

'Who's this?' asked one of the behemoths.

'Jenny Cavilleri,' answered Ray. 'Wonky music type.'

'I know that one,' said another. 'A real tight-ass.'

I ignored these crude and horny bastards as I untangled the phone and started to take it into my bedroom.

'She plays piano with the Bach Society,' said Stratton.

'What does she play with Barrett?'

'Probably hard to get!'

Oinks, grunts and guffaws. The animals were laughing.

'Gentlemen,' I announced as I took leave, 'up yours.'

I closed my door in another wave of subhuman noises, took off my shoes, lay back on the bed and dialed Jenny's number.

We spoke in whispers.

'Hey, Jen . . .'

'Yeah?'

'Jen . . . what would you say if I told you . . .'

I hesitated. She waited.

'I think . . . I'm in love with you.'

There was a pause. Then she answered very softly.

'I would say . . . you were full of shit.'

She hung up.

I wasn't unhappy. Or surprised.

III

I got hurt in the Cornell game.

It was my own fault, really. At a heated juncture, I made the unfortunate error of referring to their center as a 'fucking Canuck'. My oversight was in not remembering that four members of their team were Canadians— all, it turned out, extremely patriotic, well-built and within earshot. To add insult to injury, the penalty was called on me. And not a common one, either: five minutes for fighting. You should have heard the Cornell fans ride me when it was announced! Not many Harvard rooters had come way the hell up to Ithaca, New York, even though the Ivy title was at stake. Five minutes! I could see our coach tearing his hair out, as I climbed into the box.

Jackie Felt came scampering over. It was only then I realized that the whole right side of my face was a bloody mess. 'Jesus Christ,' he kept repeating as he worked me over with a styptic pencil. 'Jesus, Ollie.'

I sat quietly, staring blankly ahead. I was ashamed to look onto the ice, where my worst fears were quickly realized: Cornell scored. The Red fans screamed and bellowed and hooted. It was a tie now. Cornell could very possibly win the game—and with it, the Ivy title. Shit—and I had barely gone through half my penalty.

Across the rink, the minuscule Harvard contingent was grim and silent. By now the fans for both sides had forgotten me. Only one spectator still had his eyes on the penalty box. Yes, he was there. *'If the conference breaks in time, I'll try to get to Cornell.'* Sitting among the Harvard rooters—but not rooting, of course—was Oliver Barrett III.

Across the gulf of ice, Old Stonyface observed in expressionless silence as the last bit of blood on the face of his only son was stopped by adhesive papers. What was he thinking, do you think? Tch tch tch—or words to that effect?

'Oliver, if you like fighting so much, why don't you go out for the boxing team?'

'Exeter doesn't have a boxing team, Father.'

'Well, perhaps I shouldn't come up to your hockey games.'

'Do you think I fight for your benefit, Father?'

'Well, I wouldn't say "benefit".'

But of course, who could tell what he was thinking? Oliver Barrett III was a walking, sometimes talking Mount Rushmore. Stonyface.

Perhaps Old Stony was indulging in his usual self celebration: Look at me, there are extremely few Harvard spectators here this evening, and yet I am one of them. I, Oliver Barrett III, an extremely busy man with banks to run and so forth, I have taken the time to come up to Cornell for a lousy hockey game. How wonderful. (For whom?)

The crowd roared again, but really wild this time. Another Cornell goal. They were ahead. And I had two minutes of penalty to go! Davey Johnston skated up-ice, red-faced, angry. He passed right by me without so much as a glance. And did I notice tears in his eyes? I mean, okay, the title was at stake, but Jesus—tears! But then Davey, our captain, had this incredible streak going for him: seven years and he'd never played on a losing side, high school or college. It was like a minor legend. And he was a senior. And this was our last tough game.

Which we lost 6–3.

After the game, an X ray determined that no bones were broken, and then twelve stitches were sewn into my cheek by Richard Selzer, M.D. Jackie Felt hovered around the med room, telling the Cornell physician how I wasn't eating right and that all this might have been averted had I been taking sufficient salt pills. Selzer ignored Jack, and gave me a stern warning about my nearly damaging 'the floor of my orbit' (those are the medical terms) and that not to play for a week would be the wisest thing. I thanked him. He left, with Felt dogging him to talk more of nutrition. I was glad to be alone.

I showered slowly, being careful not to wet my sore face. The Novocain was wearing off a little, but I was somehow happy to feel pain. I mean, hadn't I really fucked up? We'd blown the title, broken our own streak (all the seniors had been undefeated) and Davey Johnston's too. Maybe the blame wasn't *totally* mine, but right then I felt like it was.

There was nobody in the locker room. They must all have been at the motel already. I supposed no one wanted to see me or speak to me. With this terrible bitter taste in my mouth—I felt so bad I could taste it—I packed my gear and walked outside. There were not many Harvard fans out there in the wintry wilds of upstate New York.

'How's the cheek, Barrett?'

'Okay, thanks, Mr Jencks.'

'You'll probably want a steak,' said another familiar voice. Thus spoke Oliver

Barrett III. How typical of him to suggest the old-fashioned cure for a black eye.

'Thank you, Father,' I said. 'The doctor took care of it.' I indicated the gauze pad covering Selzer's twelve stitches.

'I mean for your stomach, son.'

At dinner, we had yet another in our continuing series of nonconversations, all of which commence with 'How've you been?' and conclude with 'Anything I can do?'

'How've you been, son?'

'Fine, sir.'

'Does your face hurt?'

'No, sir.'

It was beginning to hurt like hell.

'I'd like Jack Wells to look at it on Monday.'

'Not necessary, Father.'

'He's a specialist—'

'The Cornell doctor wasn't exactly a veterinarian,' I said, hoping to dampen my father's usual snobbish enthusiasm for specialists, experts, and all other 'top people'.

'Too bad,' remarked Oliver Barrett III, in what I first took to be a stab at humor, 'you did get a *beastly* cut.'

'Yes sir,' I said. (Was I supposed to chuckle?)

And then I wondered if my father's quasi-witticism had not been intended as some sort of implicit reprimand for my actions on the ice.

'Or were you implying that I behaved like an animal this evening?'

His expression suggested some pleasure at the fact that I had asked him. But he simply replied, 'You were the one who mentioned veterinarians.' At this point, I decided to study the menu.

As the main course was served, Old Stony launched into another of his simplistic sermonettes, this one, if I recall—and I try not to—concerning victories and defeats. He noted that we had lost the title (very sharp of you, Father), but after all, in sport what really counts is not the winning but the playing. His remarks sounded suspiciously close to a paraphrase of the Olympic motto, and I sensed this was the overture to a put-down of such athletic trivia as Ivy titles. But I was not about to feed him any Olympic straight lines, so I gave him his quota of 'Yes sir's' and shut up.

We ran the usual conversational gamut, which centers around Old Stony's favorite nontopic, *my plans*.

'Tell me, Oliver, have you heard from the Law School?'

'Actually, Father, I haven't definitely decided on law school.'

'I was merely asking if law school had definitely decided on you.'

Was this another witticism? Was I supposed to smile at my father's rosy rhetoric?

'No sir. I haven't heard.'

'I could give Price Zimmermann a ring—'

'No!' I interrupted as an instant reflex. 'Please don't, sir.'

'Not to influence,' O.B. III said very uprightly, 'just to inquire.'

'Father, I want to get the letter with everyone else. Please.'

'Yes. Of course. Fine.'

'Thank you, sir.'

'Besides there really isn't much doubt about your getting in,' he added.

I don't know why, but O.B. III has a way of disparaging me even while uttering laudatory phrases.

'It's no cinch,' I replied. 'They don't have a hockey team, after all.'

I have no idea why I was putting myself down. Maybe it was because *he* was taking the opposite view.

'You have other qualities,' said Oliver

Barrett III, but declined to elaborate. (I doubt if he could have.)

The meal was as lousy as the conversation, except that I could have predicted the staleness of the rolls even before they arrived, whereas I can never predict what subject my father will set blandly before me.

'And there's always the Peace Corps,' he remarked, completely out of the blue.

'Sir?' I asked, not quite sure whether he was making a statement or asking a question.

'I think the Peace Corps is a fine thing, don't you?' he said.

'Well,' I replied, 'it's certainly better than the War Corps.'

We were even. I didn't know what he meant and vice versa. Was that it for the topic? Would we now discuss other current affairs or government programs? No. I had momentarily forgotten that our quintessential theme is always *my plans*.

'I would certainly have no objection to your joining the Peace Corps, Oliver.'

'It's mutual, sir,' I replied, matching his own generosity of spirit. I'm sure Old Stony never listens to me anyway, so I'm not surprised that he didn't react to my quiet little sarcasm.

'But among your classmates,' he continued, 'what is the attitude there?'

'Sir?'

'Do they feel the Peace Corps is relevant to their lives?'

I guess my father needs to hear the phrase as much as a fish needs water: 'Yes sir.'

Even the apple pie was stale.

At about eleven-thirty, I walked him to his car.

'Anything I can do, son?'

'No, sir. Good night, sir.'

And he drove off.

Yes, there are planes between Boston and

Ithaca, New York, but Oliver Barrett III chose to drive. Not that those many hours at the wheel could be taken as some kind of parental gesture. My father simply *likes* to drive. Fast. And at that hour of the night in an Aston Martin DBS you can go fast as hell. I have no doubt that Oliver Barrett III was out to break his Ithaca–Boston speed record, set the year previous after we had beaten Cornell and taken the title. I know, because I saw him glance at his watch.

I went back to the motel to phone Jenny.

It was the only good part of the evening. I told her all about the fight (omitting the precise nature of the *casus belli*) and I could tell she enjoyed it. Not many of her wonky musician friends either threw or received punches.

'Did you at least total the guy that hit you?' she asked.

'Yeah. Totally. I creamed him.'

'I wish I coulda seen it. Maybe you'll beat up somebody in the Yale game, huh?'

'Yeah.'

I smiled. How she loved the simple things in life.

IV

'Jenny's on the downstairs phone.'

This information was announced to me by the girl on bells, although I had not identified myself or my purpose in coming to Briggs Hall that Monday evening. I quickly concluded that this meant points for me. Obviously the 'Cliffe who greeted me read the *Crimson* and knew who I was. Okay, that had happened many times. More significant was the fact that Jenny had been mentioning that she was dating me.

'Thanks,' I said. 'I'll wait here.'

'Too bad about Cornell. The *Crime* says four guys jumped you.'

'Yeah. And *I* got the penalty. Five minutes.'

'Yeah.'

The difference between a friend and a fan is that with the latter you quickly run out of conversation. 'Jenny off the phone yet?'

She checked her switchboard, replied, 'No.'

Who could Jenny be talking to that was worth appropriating moments set aside for a date with me? Some musical wonk? It was not unknown to me that Martin Davidson, Adams House senior and conductor of the Bach Society orchestra, considered himself to have a franchise on Jenny's attention. Not body; I don't think the guy could wave more than his baton. Anyway, I would put a stop to this usurpation of *my* time.

'Where's the phone booth?'

'Around the corner.' She pointed in the precise direction.

I ambled into the lounge area. From afar I could see Jenny on the phone. She had left the booth door open. I walked slowly, casually, hoping she would catch sight of me, my bandages, my injuries in toto, and be moved to slam down the receiver and rush to my arms. As I approached, I could hear fragments of conversation.

'Yeah. Of course! Absolutely. Oh, me too, Phil. I love you too, Phil.'

I stopped ambling. Who was she talking to? It wasn't Davidson—there was no Phil in any part of his name. I had long ago checked him out in our Class Register: *Martin Eugene Davidson, 70 Riverside Drive, New York. High*

School of Music and Art. His photo suggested sensitivity, intelligence and about fifty pounds less than me. But why was I bothering about Davidson? Clearly both he and I were being shot down by Jennifer Cavilleri, for someone to whom she was at this moment (how gross!) blowing kisses into the phone!

I had been away only forty-eight hours, and some bastard named Phil had crawled into bed with Jenny (it had to be that!).

'Yeah, Phil, I love you too. Bye.'

As she was hanging up, she saw me, and without so much as blushing, she smiled and waved me a kiss. How could she be so two-faced?

She kissed me lightly on my unhurt cheek.

'Hey—you look awful.'

'I'm injured, Jen.'

'Does the other guy look worse?'

'Yeah. Much. I always make the other guy look worse.'

I said that as ominously as I could, sort of implying that I would punch-out any rivals who would creep into bed with Jenny while I was out of sight and evidently out of mind. She grabbed my sleeve and we started toward the door.

'Night, Jenny,' called the girl on bells.

'Night, Sara Jane,' Jenny called back.

When we were outside, about to step into my MG, I oxygenated my lungs with a breath of evening, and put the question as casually as I could.

'Say, Jen . . .'

'Yeah?'

'Uh—who's Phil?'

She answered matter-of-factly as she got into the car:

'My father.'

I wasn't about to believe a story like that.

'You call your father Phil?'

'That's his name. What do you call yours?'

Jenny had once told me she had been raised by her father, some sort of a baker type, in Cranston, Rhode Island. When she was very young, her mother was killed in a car crash. All this by way of explaining why she had no driver's license. Her father, in every other way 'a truly good guy' (her words), was incredibly superstitious about letting his only daughter drive. This was a real drag during her last years of high school, when she was taking piano with a guy in Providence. But then she got to read all of Proust on those long bus rides.

'What do you call yours?' she asked again.

I had been so out of it, I hadn't heard her question.

'My what?'

'What term do you employ when you speak of your progenitor?'

I answered with the term I'd always wanted to employ.

'Sonovabitch.'

'To his face?' she asked.

'I never see his face.'

'He wears a mask?'

'In a way, yes. Of stone. Of absolute stone.'

'Go on—he must be proud as hell. You're a big Harvard jock.'

I looked at her. I guess she didn't know everything, after all.

'So was he, Jenny.'

'Bigger than All-Ivy wing?'

I liked the way she enjoyed my athletic credentials. Too bad I had to shoot myself down by giving her my father's.

'He rowed single sculls in the 1928 Olympics.'

'God,' she said. 'Did he win?'

'No,' I answered, and I guess she could tell that the fact that he was sixth in the finals actually afforded me some comfort.

There was a little silence. Now maybe Jenny would understand that to be Oliver Barrett IV doesn't just mean living with that gray stone edifice in Harvard Yard. It involves a kind of muscular intimidation as well. I mean, the image of athletic achievement looming down on you. I mean, on me.

'But what does he do to qualify as a sonovabitch?' Jenny asked.

'Make me,' I replied.

'Beg pardon?'

'*Make* me,' I repeated.

Her eyes widened like saucers. 'You mean like *incest*?' she asked.

'Don't give me your family problems, Jen. I've got enough of my own.'

'Like what, Oliver?' she asked. 'Like just what *is* it he makes you do?'

'The "right things",' I said.

'What's wrong with the "right things"?' she asked, delighting in the apparent paradox.

I told her how I loathed being programmed for the Barrett Tradition—which she should have realized, having seen me cringe at having to mention the numeral at the end of my name. And I did not like having to deliver x amount of achievement every single term.

'Oh yeah,' said Jenny with broad sarcasm, 'I notice how you hate getting A's, being All-Ivy—'

'What I hate is that he expects no less!' Just saying what I had always felt (but never before spoken) made me feel uncomfortable as hell, but now I had to make Jenny understand it all. 'And he's so incredibly blasé when I do come through. I mean he just takes me absolutely for granted.'

'But he's a busy man. Doesn't he run lots of banks and things?'

'Jesus, Jenny, whose side are you on?'

'Is this a war?' she asked.

'Most definitely,' I replied.

'That's ridiculous, Oliver.'

She seemed genuinely unconvinced. And there I got my first inkling of a cultural gap between us. I mean, three and a half years of Harvard-Radcliffe had pretty much made us into the cocky intellectuals that institution traditionally produces, but when it came to accepting the fact that my father was made of stone, she adhered to some atavistic Italian-Mediterranean notion of papa-loves-bambinos, and there was no arguing otherwise.

I tried to cite a case in point: that ridiculous nonconversation after the Cornell game. This definitely made an impression on her. But the goddamn wrong one.

'He went all the way up to Ithaca to watch a lousy hockey game?'

I tried to explain that my father was all form and no content. She was still obsessed with the fact that he had traveled so far for such a (relatively) trivial sports event.

'Look, Jenny, can we just forget it?'

'Thank God you're hung up about your father,' she replied. 'That means you're not perfect.'

'Oh—you mean *you* are?'

'Hell no, Preppie. If I was, would I be going out with you?'

Back to business as usual.

V

I would like to say a word about our physical relationship.

For a strangely long while there wasn't any. I mean, there wasn't anything more significant than those kisses already mentioned (all of which I still remember in greatest detail). This was not standard procedure as far as I was concerned, being rather impulsive, impatient and quick to action. If you were to tell any of a dozen girls at Tower Court, Wellesley, that Oliver Barrett IV had been dating a young lady *daily* for three weeks and had not slept with her, they would surely have laughed and severely questioned the femininity of the girl involved. But of course the actual facts were quite different.

I didn't know what to do.

Don't misunderstand or take that too literally. I knew all the moves. I just couldn't cope with my own feelings about making them. Jenny was so smart that I was afraid she might laugh at what I had traditionally considered the suave romantic (and unstoppable) style of Oliver Barrett IV. I was afraid of being rejected, yes. I was also afraid of being accepted for the wrong reasons. What I am fumbling to say is that I felt different about Jennifer, and didn't know what to say or even who to ask about it. ('You should have asked me,' she said later.) I just knew I had these feelings. For her. For all of her.

'You're gonna flunk out, Oliver.'

We were sitting in my room on a Sunday afternoon, reading.

'Oliver, you're gonna flunk out if you just sit there watching me study.'

'I'm not watching you study. I'm studying.'

'Bullshit. You're looking at my legs.'

'Only once in a while. Every chapter.'

'That book has extremely short chapters.'

'Listen, you narcissistic bitch, you're not *that* great-looking!'

'I know. But can I help it if you think so?'

I threw down my book and crossed the room to where she was sitting.

'Jenny, for Christ's sake, how can I read John Stuart Mill when every single second I'm dying to make love to you?'

She screwed up her brow and frowned.

'Oh, Oliver, wouldja please?'

I was crouching by her chair. She looked back into her book.

'Jenny—'

She closed her book softly, put it down, then placed her hands on the sides of my neck.

'Oliver—wouldja please.'

It all happened at once. Everything. Our first physical encounter was the polar opposite of our first verbal one. It was all so unhurried, so soft, so gentle. I had never realized that this was the real Jenny the soft one, whose touch was so light and so loving. And yet what truly shocked me was my own response. *I* was gentle. *I* was tender. Was this the real Oliver Barrett IV?

As I said, I had never seen Jenny with so much as her sweater opened an extra button. I was somewhat surprised to find that she wore a tiny golden cross. On one of those chains that never unlock. Meaning that when we made love, she still wore the cross. In a resting moment of that lovely afternoon, at one of those junctures when everything and nothing is relevant, I touched the little cross and inquired what her priest might have to say about our being in bed together, and so forth. She answered that she had no priest.

'Aren't you a good Catholic girl?' I asked.

'Well, I'm a girl,' she said. 'And I'm good.'

She looked at me for confirmation and I smiled. She smiled back.

'So that's two out of three.'

I then asked her why the cross, welded, no less. She explained that it had been her mother's; she wore it for sentimental reasons, not religious. The conversation returned to ourselves.

'Hey, Oliver, did I tell you that I love you?' she said.

'No, Jen.'

'Why didn't you ask me?'

'I was afraid to, frankly.'

'Ask me now.'

'Do you love me, Jenny?'

She looked at me and wasn't being evasive when she answered:

'What do you think?'

'Yeah. I guess. Maybe.'

I kissed her neck.

'Oliver?'

'Yes?'

'I don't just love you . . .'

Oh, Christ, what was this?

'I love you very much, Oliver.'

VI

I love Ray Stratton.

He may not be a genius or a great football player (kind of slow at the snap), but he was always a good roommate and loyal friend. And how that poor bastard suffered through most of our senior year. Where did he go to study when he saw the tie placed on the door-knob of our room (the traditional signal for 'action within')? Admittedly, he didn't study that much, but he had to *sometimes*. Let's say he used the House library, or Lamont, or even the Pi Eta Club. But where did he sleep on those Saturday nights when Jenny and I decided to disobey parietal rules and stay together? Ray had to scrounge for places to sack in—neighbors' couches, etc., assuming *they* had nothing going for them. Well, at least it was after the foot-ball season. And I would have done the same thing for him.

But what was Ray's reward? In days of yore I had shared with him the minutest details of my amorous triumphs. Now he was not only denied these inalienable roommate's rights, but I never even came out and admitted that Jenny and I were lovers. I would just indicate when we would be needing the room, and so forth. Stratton could draw what conclusion he wished.

'I mean, Christ, Barrett, are you making it or not?' he would ask.

'Raymond, as a friend I'm asking you not to ask.'

'But Christ, Barrett, afternoons, Friday nights, Saturday nights. Christ, you *must* be making it.'

'Then why bother asking me, Ray?'

'Because it's unhealthy.'

'What is?'

'The whole situation, Ol. I mean, it was never like this before. I mean, this total freeze-out on details for big Ray. I mean, this is unwarranted. Unhealthy. Christ, what does she do that's so different?'

'Look, Ray, in a mature love affair—'

'Love?'

'Don't say it like it's a dirty word.'

'At your age? Love? Christ, I greatly fear, old buddy.'

'For what? My sanity?'

'Your bachelorhood. Your freedom. Your life!'

Poor Ray. He really meant it.

'Afraid you're losing a roommate, huh?'

'Shit, in a way I've *gained* one, she spends so much time here.'

I was dressing for a concert, so this dialogue would shortly come to a close.

'Don't sweat, Raymond. We'll have that apartment in New York. Different babies every night. We'll do it all.'

'Don't tell me not to sweat, Barrett. That girl's *got* you.'

'It's all under control,' I replied. 'Stay loose.' I was adjusting my tie and heading for the door. Stratton was somehow unconvinced.

'Hey, Ollie?'

'Yeah?'

'You are making it, aren't you?'

'Jesus Christ, Stratton!'

I was not taking Jenny to this concert; I was *watching* her in it. The Bach Society was doing the Fifth Brandenburg Concerto at Dunster House, and Jenny was harpsichord soloist. I had heard her play many times, of course, but never with a group or in public. Christ, was I proud. She didn't make any mistakes that I could notice.

'I can't believe how great you were,' I said after the concert.

'That shows what you know about music, Preppie.'

'I know enough.'

We were in the Dunster courtyard. It was one of those April afternoons when you'd believe spring might finally reach Cambridge. Her musical colleagues were strolling nearby (including Martin Davidson, throwing invisible hate bombs in my direction), so I couldn't argue keyboard expertise with her.

We crossed Memorial Drive to walk along the river.

'Wise up, Barrett, wouldja please. I play

okay. Not great. Not even "All-Ivy". Just okay. Okay?'

How could I argue when she wanted to put herself down?

'Okay. You play okay. I just mean you should always keep at it.'

'Who said I wasn't going to keep at it, for God's sake? I'm gonna study with Nadia Boulanger, aren't I?'

What the hell was she talking about? From the way she immediately shut up, I sensed this was something she had not intended to mention.

'Who?' I asked.

'Nadia Boulanger. A famous music teacher. In Paris.' She said those last two words rather quickly.

'In Paris?' I asked, rather slowly.

'She takes very few American pupils. I was lucky. I got a good scholarship too.'

'Jennifer—you are going to Paris?'

'I've never seen Europe. I can hardly wait.'

I grabbed her by the shoulders. Maybe I was too rough. I don't know.

'Hey—how long have you known this?'

For once in her life, Jenny couldn't look me square in the eye.

'Ollie, don't be stupid,' she said. 'It's inevitable.'

'What's inevitable?'

'We graduate and we go our separate ways. You'll go to law school—'

'Wait a minute—what are you talking about?'

Now she looked me in the eye. And her face was sad.

'Ollie, you're a preppie millionaire, and I'm a social zero.'

I was still holding onto her shoulders.

'What the hell does that have to do with separate ways? We're together now, we're happy.'

'Ollie, don't be stupid,' she repeated. 'Harvard is like Santa's Christmas bag. You can stuff any crazy kind of toy into it. But when the holiday's over, they shake you out . . .' She hesitated.

'. . . and you gotta go back where you belong.'

'You mean you're going to bake cookies in Cranston, Rhode Island?'

I was saying desperate things.

'Pastries,' she said. 'And don't make fun of my father.'

'Then don't leave me, Jenny. *Please.*'

'What about my scholarship? What about Paris, which I've never seen in my whole goddamn life?'

'What about our marriage?'

It was I who spoke those words, although for a split second I wasn't sure I really had.

'Who said anything about marriage?'

'Me. I'm saying it now.'

'You want to marry me?'

'Yes.'

She tilted her head, did not smile, but merely inquired:

'Why?'

I looked her straight in the eye.

'Because,' I said.

'Oh,' she said. 'That's a very good reason.'

She took my arm (not my sleeve this time), and we walked along the river. There was nothing more to say, really.

VII

Ipswich, Mass., is some forty minutes from the Mystic River Bridge, depending on the weather and how you drive. I have actually made it on occasion in twenty-nine minutes. A certain distinguished Boston banker claims an even faster time, but when one is discussing sub thirty minutes from Bridge to Barretts', it is difficult to separate fact from fancy. I happen to consider twenty-nine minutes as the absolute limit. I mean, you can't ignore the traffic signals on Route I, can you?

'You're driving like a maniac,' Jenny said.

'This is Boston,' I replied. 'Everyone drives like a maniac.' We were halted for a red light on Route I at the time.

'You'll kill us before your parents can murder us.'

'Listen, Jen, my parents are lovely people.'

The light changed. The MG was at sixty in under ten seconds.

'Even the Sonovabitch?' she asked.

'Who?'

'Oliver Barrett III.'

'Ah, he's a nice guy. You'll really like him.'

'How do you know?'

'Everybody likes him,' I replied.

'Then why don't you?'

'Because everybody likes him,' I said.

Why was I taking her to meet them,

anyway? I mean, did I really need Old Stonyface's blessing or anything? Part of it was that she wanted to ('That's the way it's done, Oliver') and part of it was the simple fact that Oliver III was my banker in the very grossest sense: he paid the goddamn tuition.

It had to be Sunday dinner, didn't it? I mean, that's *comme il faut*, right? Sunday, when all the lousy drivers were clogging Route 1 and getting in my way. I pulled off the main drag onto Groton Street, a road whose turns I had been taking at high speeds since I was thirteen.

'There are no houses here,' said Jenny, 'just trees.'

'The houses are behind the trees.'

When traveling down Groton Street, you've got to be very careful or else you'll miss the turnoff into our place. Actually, I missed the turnoff myself that afternoon. I was three hundred yards down the road when I screeched to a halt.

'Where are we?' she asked.

'Past it,' I mumbled, between obscenities.

Is there something symbolic in the fact that I backed up three hundred yards to the entrance of our place? Anyway, I drove slowly once we were on Barrett soil. It's at least a half mile in from Groton Street to Dover House proper. En route you pass other . . . well, buildings. I guess it's fairly impressive when you see it for the first time.

'Holy shit!' Jenny said.

'What's the matter, Jen?'

'Pull over, Oliver. No kidding. Stop the car.'

I stopped the car. She was clutching.

'Hey, I didn't think it would be like this.'

'Like what?'

'Like this rich. I mean, I bet you have *serfs* living here.'

I wanted to reach over and touch her, but my palms were not dry (an uncommon state), and so I gave her verbal reassurance.

'Please, Jen. It'll be a breeze.'

'Yeah, but why is it I suddenly wish my name was Abigail Adams, or Wendy WASP?'

We drove the rest of the way in silence, parked and walked up to the front door. As he waited for the ring to be answered, Jenny succumbed to a last-minute panic.

'Let's run,' she said.

'Let's stay and fight,' I said.

Was either of us joking?

The door was opened by Florence, a devoted and antique servant of the Barrett family.

'Ah, Master Oliver,' she greeted me.

God, how I hate to be called that! I detest that implicitly derogatory distinction between me and Old Stonyface.

My parents, Florence informed us, were

waiting in the library. Jenny was taken aback by some of the portraits we passed. Not just that some were by John Singer Sargent (notably Oliver Barrett II, sometimes displayed in the Boston Museum), but the new realization that not all of my forebears were named Barrett. There had been solid Barrett *women* who had mated well and bred such creatures as Barrett Winthrop, Richard Barrett Sewall and even Abbott Lawrence Lyman, who had the temerity to go through life (and Harvard, its implicit analogue), becoming a prizewinning chemist, without so much as a Barrett in his middle name!

'Jesus Christ,' said Jenny. 'I see half the buildings at Harvard hanging here.'

'It's all crap,' I told her.

'I didn't know you were related to Sewall Boat House too,' she said.

'Yeah. I come from a long line of wood and stone.'

At the end of the long row of portraits, and just before one turns into the library, stands a glass case. In the case are trophies. Athletic trophies.

'They're gorgeous,' Jenny said. 'I've never seen ones that look like real gold and silver.'

'They are.'

'Jesus. Yours?'

'No. His.'

It is an indisputable matter of record that Oliver Barrett III did not place in the Amsterdam Olympics. It is, however, also quite true that he enjoyed significant rowing triumphs on various other occasions. Several. Many. The well-polished proof of this was now before Jennifer's dazzled eyes.

'They don't give stuff like that in the Cranston bowling leagues.'

Then I think she tossed me a bone.

'Do you have trophies, Oliver?'

'Yes.'

'In a case?'

'Up in my room. Under the bed.'

She gave me one of her good Jenny-looks and whispered:

'We'll go look at them later, huh?'

Before I could answer, or even gauge Jenny's true motivations for suggesting a trip to my bedroom, we were interrupted.

'Ah, hello there.'

Sonovabitch! It was the Sonovabitch.

'Oh, hello, sir. This is Jennifer—'

'Ah, hello there.'

He was shaking her hand before I could finish the introduction. I noted that he was not wearing any of his Banker Costumes. No indeed; Oliver III had on a fancy cashmere sport jacket. And there was an insidious smile on his usually rock-like countenance.

'Do come in and meet Mrs Barrett.'

Another once-in-a-lifetime thrill was in store for Jennifer: meeting Alison Forbes

'Tipsy' Barrett. (In perverse moments I wondered how her boardingschool nickname might have affected her, had she not grown up to be the earnest do-gooder museum trustee she was.) Let the record show that Tipsy Forbes never completed college. She left Smith in her sophomore year, with the full blessing of her parents, to wed Oliver Barrett III.

'My wife Alison, this is Jennifer—'

He had already usurped the function of introducing her.

'Calliveri,' I added, since Old Stony didn't know her last name.

'Cavilleri,' Jenny added politely, since I had mispronounced it—for the first and only time in my goddamn life.

'As in *Cavalleria Rusticana*?' asked my mother, probably to prove that despite her drop-out status, she was still pretty cultured.

'Right.' Jenny smiled at her. 'No relation.'

'Ah,' said my mother.

'Ah,' said my father.

To which, all the time wondering if they had caught Jenny's humor, I could but add: 'Ah?'

Mother and Jenny shook hands, and after the usual exchange of banalities from which one never progressed in my house, we sat down. Everybody was quiet. I tried to sense what was happening. Doubtless, Mother was sizing up Jennifer, checking out her costume (not Boho this afternoon), her posture, her demeanor, her accent. Face it, the Sound of Cranston was there even in the politest of moments. Perhaps Jenny was sizing up Mother. Girls do that, I'm told. It's supposed to reveal things about the guys they're going to marry. Maybe she was also sizing up Oliver III. Did she notice he was taller than I? Did she like his cashmere jacket?

Oliver III, of course, would be concentrating his fire on me, as usual.

'How've you been, son?'

75

For a goddamn Rhodes scholar, he is one lousy conversationalist.

'Fine, sir. Fine.'

As a kind of equal-time gesture, Mother greeted Jennifer.

'Did you have a nice trip down?'

'Yes,' Jenny replied, 'nice and swift.'

'Oliver is a swift driver,' interposed Old Stony.

'No swifter than you, Father,' I retorted.

What would he say to that?

'Uh—yes. I suppose not.'

You bet your ass not, Father.

Mother, who is always on his side, whatever the circumstances, turned the subject to one of more universal interest—music or art, I believe. I wasn't exactly listening carefully. Subsequently, a teacup found its way into my hand.

'Thank you,' I said, then added, 'We'll have to be going soon.'

'Huh?' said Jenny. It seems they had been discussing Puccini or something, and my remark was considered somewhat tangential. Mother looked at me (a rare event).

'But you did come for dinner, didn't you?'

'Uh—we can't,' I said.

'Of course,' Jenny said, almost at the same time.

'I've gotta get back,' I said earnestly to Jen.

Jenny gave me a look of 'What are you talking about?'. Then Old Stonyface pronounced:

'You're staying for dinner. That's an order.'

The fake smile on his face didn't make it any less of a command. And I don't take that kind of crap even from an Olympic finalist.

'We can't, sir,' I replied.

'We have to, Oliver,' said Jenny.

'Why?' I asked.

'Because I'm hungry,' she said.

We sat at the table obedient to the wishes of Oliver III. He bowed his head. Mother and Jenny followed suit. I tilted mine slightly.

'Bless this food to our use and us to Thy service, and help us to be ever mindful of the needs and wants of others. This we ask in the name of Thy Son Jesus Christ, Amen.'

Jesus Christ, I was mortified. Couldn't he have omitted the piety just this once? What would Jenny think? God, it was a throwback to the Dark Ages.

'Amen,' said Mother (and Jenny too, very softly).

'Play ball!' said I, as kind of a pleasantry.

Nobody seemed amused. Least of all Jenny. She looked away from me. Oliver III glanced across at me.

'I certainly wish you would play ball now and then, Oliver.'

We did not eat in total silence, thanks to my mother's remarkable capacity for small talk.

'So your people are from Cranston, Jenny?'

'Mostly. My mother was from Fall River.'

'The Barretts have mills in Fall River,' noted Oliver III.

'Where they exploited the poor for generations,' added Oliver IV.

'In the nineteenth century,' added Oliver III.

My mother smiled at this, apparently satisfied that *her* Oliver had taken that set. But not so.

'What about those plans to automate the mills?' I volleyed back.

There was a brief pause. I awaited some slamming retort.

'What about coffee?' said Alison Forbes Tipsy Barrett.

We withdrew into the library for what would definitely be the last round. Jenny and I had classes the next day, Stony had the bank and so forth, and surely Tipsy would have something worthwhile planned for bright and early.

'Sugar, Oliver?' asked my mother.

'Oliver always takes sugar, dear,' said my father.

'Not tonight, thank you,' said I. 'Just black, Mother.'

Well, we all had our cups, and we were all sitting there cozily with absolutely nothing to say to one another. So I brought up a topic.

'Tell me, Jennifer,' I inquired. 'What do you think of the Peace Corps?'

She frowned at me, and refused to cooperate.

'Oh, have you told them, O.B.?' said my mother to my father.

'It isn't the time, dear,' said Oliver III, with a kind of fake humility that broadcasted, 'Ask me, ask me.' So I had to.

'What's this, Father?'

'Nothing important, son.'

'I don't see how you can say that,' said my

mother, and turned toward me to deliver the message with full force (I said she was on his side):

'Your father's going to be director of the Peace Corps.'

'Oh.'

Jenny also said, 'Oh,' but in a different, kind of happier tone of voice.

My father pretended to look embarrassed, and my mother seemed to be waiting for me to bow down or something. I mean, it's not Secretary of State, after all!

'Congratulations, Mr Barrett.' Jenny took the initiative.

'Yes. Congratulations, sir.'

Mother was so anxious to talk about it.

'I do think it will be a wonderful educational experience,' she said.

'Oh, it will,' agreed Jenny.

'Yes,' I said without much conviction. 'Uh—would you pass the sugar, please.'

VIII

'Jenny, it's not Secretary of State, after all!'

We were finally driving back to Cambridge, thank God.

'Still, Oliver, you could have been more enthusiastic.'

'I said congratulations.'

'It was mighty generous of you.'

'What did you expect, for chrissake?'

'Oh, God,' she replied, 'the whole thing makes me sick.'

'That's two of us,' I added.

We drove on for a long time without saying a word. But something was wrong.

'What whole thing makes you sick, Jen?' I asked as a long afterthought.

'The disgusting way you treat your father.'

'How about the disgusting way he treats me?'

I had opened a can of beans. Or, more appropriately, spaghetti sauce. For Jenny launched into a full-scale offense on paternal love. That whole Italian-Mediterranean syndrome. And how I was disrespectful.

'You bug him and bug him and bug him,' she said.

'It's mutual, Jen. Or didn't you notice that?'

'I don't think you'd stop at anything, just to get to your old man.'

'It's impossible to "get to" Oliver Barrett III.'

There was a strange little silence before she replied:

'Unless maybe if you marry Jennifer Cavilleri . . .'

I kept my cool long enough to pull into the parking lot of a seafood diner. I then turned to Jennifer, mad as hell.

'Is that what you think?' I demanded.

'I think it's part of it,' she said very quietly.

'Jenny, don't you believe I love you?' I shouted.

'Yes,' she replied, still quietly, 'but in a crazy way you also love my negative social status.'

I couldn't think of anything to say but no. I said it several times and in several tones of voice. I mean, I was so terribly upset, I even considered the possibility of there being a grain of truth to her awful suggestion.

But she wasn't in great shape, either.

'I can't pass judgment, Ollie. I just think it's part of it. I mean, I know I love not only you yourself. I love your name. And your numeral.'

She looked away, and I thought maybe she was going to cry. But she didn't; she finished her thought:

'After all, it's part of what you are.'

I sat there for a while, watching a neon sign blink 'Clams and Oysters.' What I had loved so much about Jenny was her ability to see inside me, to understand things I never needed to carve out in words. She was still doing it. But could I face the fact that I wasn't perfect? Christ, she had already faced my imperfection *and her own*. Christ, how unworthy I felt!

I didn't know what the hell to say.

'Would you like a clam or an oyster, Jen?'

'Would you like a punch in the mouth, Preppie?'

'Yes,' I said.

She made a fist and then placed it gently against my cheek. I kissed it, and as I reached over to embrace her, she straight-armed me, and barked like a gun moll:

'Just drive, Preppie. Get back to the wheel and start speeding!'

I did. I did.

My father's basic comment concerned what he considered excessive velocity. Haste. Precipitousness. I forget his exact words, but I know the text for his sermon during our luncheon at the Harvard Club concerned itself primarily with my going too fast. He warmed up for it by suggesting that I not bolt my food. I politely suggested that I was a grown man, that he should no longer correct—or even comment upon—my behaviour. He allowed that even world leaders needed constructive criticism now and then. I took this to be a not-too-subtle allusion to his stint in Washington during the first Roosevelt Administration. But I was not about to set him up to reminisce about F.D.R., or his role in U.S. bank reform. So I shut up.

We were, as I said, eating lunch in the Harvard Club of Boston. (I too fast, if one accepts my father's estimate.) This means we were surrounded by his people. His classmates, clients, admirers and so forth. I mean, it was a put-up job, if ever there was one. If you really listened, you might hear some of them murmur things like, 'There goes Oliver Barrett.' Or 'That's Barrett, the big athlete.'

It was yet another round in our series of nonconversations. Only the very nonspecific nature of the talk was glaringly conspicuous.

'Father, you haven't said a word about Jennifer.'

'What is there to say? You've presented us with a fait accompli, have you not?'

'But what do you *think*, Father?'

'I think Jennifer is admirable. And for a girl from her background to get all the way to Radcliffe . . .'

With this pseudo-melting-pot bullshit, he was skirting the issue.

'Get to the point, Father!'

'The point has nothing to do with the young lady,' he said, 'it has to do with you.'

'Ah?' I said.

'Your rebellion,' he added. 'You are rebelling, son.'

'Father, I fail to see how marrying a beautiful and brilliant Radcliffe girl constitutes rebellion. I mean, she's not some crazy hippie—'

'She is not many things.'

Ah, here we come. The goddamn nitty gritty.

'What irks you most, Father—that she's Catholic or that she's poor?'

He replied in kind of a whisper, leaning slightly toward me.

'What *attracts* you most?'

I wanted to get up and leave. I told him so.

'Stay here and talk like a man,' he said.

As opposed to what? A boy? A girl? A mouse? Anyway, I stayed.

The Sonovabitch derived enormous satisfaction from my remaining seated. I mean, I could tell he regarded it as another in his many victories over me.

'I would only ask that you wait awhile,' said Oliver Barrett III.

'Define "while", please.'

'Finish law school. If this is real, it can stand the test of time.'

'It *is* real, but why in hell should I subject it to some arbitrary test?'

My implication was clear, I think. I was standing up to him. To his arbitrariness. To his compulsion to dominate and control my life.

'Oliver.' He began a new round. 'You're a minor—'

'A minor *what*?' I was losing my temper, goddammit.

'You are not yet twenty-one. Not legally an adult.'

'Screw the legal nitpicking, dammit!'

Perhaps some neighboring diners heard this remark. As if to compensate for my loudness, Oliver III aimed his next words at me in a biting whisper:

'Marry her now, and I will not give you the time of day.' Who gave a shit if somebody overheard.

'Father, you don't *know* the time of day.'

I walked out of his life and began my own.

IX

There remained the matter of Cranston, Rhode Island, a city slightly more to the south of Boston than Ipswich is to the north. After the debacle of introducing Jennifer to her potential in-laws ('Do I call them outlaws now?' she asked), I did not look forward with any confidence to my meeting with her father. I mean, here I would be bucking that lotsa love Italian-Mediterranean syndrome, compounded by the fact that Jenny was an only child, compounded by the fact that she had no mother, which meant abnormally close ties to her father. I would be up against all those emotional forces the psych books describe.

Plus the fact that I was broke.

I mean, imagine for a second Olivero Barretto, some nice Italian kid from down the block in Cranston, Rhode Island. He comes to see Mr Cavilleri, a wage-earning pastry chef of that city, and says, 'I would like to marry your only daughter, Jennifer.' What would the old man's first question be? (He would not question Barretto's love, since to know Jenny is to love Jenny; it's a universal truth.) No, Mr Cavilleri would say something like, 'Barretto, how are you going to support her?'

Now imagine the good Mr Cavilleri's reaction if Barretto informed him that the opposite would prevail, at least for the next three years: his daughter would have to support his son-in-law! Would not the good Mr Cavilleri show Barretto to the door, or even, if Barretto were not my size, punch him out?

You bet your ass he would.

This may serve to explain why, on that Sunday afternoon in May, I was obeying all posted speed limits, as we headed southward on Route 95. Jenny, who had come to enjoy the pace at which I drove, complained at one point that I was going forty in a forty-five-mile-an-hour zone. I told her the car needed tuning, which she believed not at all.

'Tell it to me again, Jen.'

Patience was not one of Jenny's virtues, and she refused to bolster my confidence by repeating the answers to all the stupid questions I had asked.

'Just one more time, Jenny, please.'

'I called him. I told him. He said okay. In English, because, as I told you and you don't seem to want to believe, he doesn't know a goddamn word of Italian except a few curses.'

'But what does "okay" *mean*?'

'Are you implying that Harvard Law School has accepted a man who can't even define "okay"?'

'It's not a legal term, Jenny.'

She touched my arm. Thank God, I understood that. I still needed clarification, though. I had to know what I was in for.

'"Okay" could also mean "I'll *suffer* through it".'

She found the charity in her heart to repeat for the nth time the details of her conversation with her father. He was happy. He *was*. He had never expected, when he sent her off to Radcliffe, that she would return to Cranston to marry the boy next door (who by the way had asked her just before she left). He was at first incredulous that her intended's name was really Oliver Barrett IV. He had then warned his daughter not to violate the Eleventh Commandment.

'Which one is that?' I asked her.

'Do not bullshit thy father,' she said.

'Oh.'

'And that's all, Oliver. Truly.'

'He knows I'm poor?'

'Yes.'

'He doesn't mind?'

'At least you and he have something in common.'

'But he'd be happier if I had a few bucks, right?'

'Wouldn't you?'

I shut up for the rest of the ride.

* * *

Jenny lived on a street called Hamilton Avenue, a long line of wooden houses with many children in front of them, and a few scraggly trees. Merely driving down it, looking for a parking space, I felt like in another country. To begin with, there were so many people. Besides the children playing, there were entire families sitting on their porches with apparently nothing better to do this Sunday afternoon than to watch me park my MG.

Jenny leaped out first. She had incredible reflexes in Cranston, like some quick little grasshopper. There was all but an organized cheer when the porch watchers saw who my passenger was. No less than the great Cavilleri! When I heard all the greetings for her, I was almost ashamed to get out. I mean, I could not remotely for a moment pass for the hypothetical Olivero Barretto.

'Hey, Jenny!' I heard one matronly type shout with great gusto.

'Hey, Mrs Capodilupo,' I heard Jenny

bellow back. I climbed out of the car. I could feel the eyes on me.

'Hey—who's the boy?' shouted Mrs Capodilupo. Not too subtle around here, are they?

'He's nothing!' Jenny called back. Which did wonders for my confidence.

'Maybe,' shouted Mrs Capodilupo in my direction, 'but the girl he's with is really something!'

'He knows,' Jenny replied.

She then turned to satisfy neighbors on the *other* side.

'He knows,' she told a whole new group of her fans.

She took my hand (I was a stranger in paradise), and led me up the stairs to 189A Hamilton Avenue.

It was an awkward moment.

I just stood there as Jenny said, 'This is my

father.' And Phil Cavilleri, a roughhewn (say 5' 9", 165-pound) Rhode Island type in his late forties, held out his hand.

We shook and he had a strong grip.

'How do you do, sir?'

'Phil,' he corrected me, 'I'm Phil.'

'Phil, sir,' I replied, continuing to shake his hand.

It was also a scary moment. Because then, just as he let go of my hand, Mr Cavilleri turned to his daughter and gave this incredible shout:

'Jennifer!'

For a split second nothing happened. And then they were hugging. Tight. Very tight. Rocking to and fro. All Mr Cavilleri could offer by way of further comment was the (now very soft) repetition of his daughter's name: 'Jennifer.' And all his graduating-Radcliffe-with-honors daughter could offer by way of reply was: 'Phil.'

I was definitely the odd man out.

One thing about my couth upbringing helped me out that afternoon. I had always been lectured about not talking with my mouth full. Since Phil and his daughter kept conspiring to fill that orifice, I didn't have to speak. I must have eaten a record quantity of Italian pastries. Afterward I discoursed at some length on which ones I had liked best (I ate no less than two of each kind, for fear of giving offense), to the delight of the two Cavilleris.

'He's okay,' said Phil Cavilleri to his daughter.

What did that mean?

I didn't need to have 'okay' defined; I merely wished to know what of my few and circumspect actions had earned for me that cherished epithet.

Did I like the right cookies? Was my handshake strong enough? What?

'I *told* you he was okay, Phil,' said Mr Cavilleri's daughter.

'Well, okay,' said her father, 'I still had to see for myself. Now I saw. Oliver?'

He was now addressing me.

'Yes, sir?'

'Phil.'

'Yes, Phil, sir?'

'You're okay.'

'Thank you, sir. I appreciate it. Really I do. And you know how I feel about your daughter, sir. And you, sir.'

'Oliver,' Jenny interrupted, 'will you stop babbling like a stupid goddamn preppie, and—'

'Jennifer,' Mr Cavilleri interrupted, 'can you avoid the profanity? The sonovabitch is a guest!'

At dinner (the pastries turned out to be merely a snack) Phil tried to have a serious talk with me about you-can-guess-what. For some crazy reason he thought he could effect a rapprochement between Olivers III and IV.

'Let me speak to him on the phone, father to father,' he pleaded.

'Please, Phil, it's a waste of time.'

'I can't sit here and allow a parent to reject a child. I can't.'

'Yeah. But I reject him too, Phil.'

'Don't ever let me hear you talk like that,' he said, getting genuinely angry. 'A father's love is to be cherished and respected. It's rare.'

'Especially in my family,' I said.

Jenny was getting up and down to serve, so she was not involved with most of this.

'Get him on the phone,' Phil repeated. 'I'll take care of this.'

'No, Phil. My father and I have installed a cold line.'

'Aw, listen, Oliver, he'll thaw. Believe me when I tell you he'll thaw. When it's time to go to church—'

At this moment Jenny, who was handing out dessert plates, directed at her father a portentous monosyllable.

'Phil . . . ?'

'Yeah, Jen?'

'About the church bit . . .'

'Yeah?'

'Uh—kind of negative on it, Phil.'

'Oh?' asked Mr Cavilleri. Then, leaping instantly to the wrong conclusion, he turned apologetically toward me.

'I—uh—didn't mean necessarily Catholic Church, Oliver. I mean, as Jennifer has no doubt told you, we are of the Catholic faith. But, I mean, *your church*, Oliver. God will bless this union in any church, I swear.'

I looked at Jenny, who had obviously failed to cover this crucial topic in her phone conversation.

'Oliver,' she explained, 'it was just too goddamn much to hit him with at once.'

'What's this?' asked the ever affable Mr Cavilleri. 'Hit me, hit me, children. I want to be hit with everything on your minds.'

Why is it that at this precise moment my eyes hit upon the porcelain statue of the Virgin Mary on a shelf in the Cavilleris' dining room?

'It's about the God-blessing bit, Phil,' said Jenny, averting her gaze from him.

'Yeah, Jen, yeah?' asked Phil, fearing the worst.

'Uh—kind of negative on it, Phil,' she said, now glancing at me for support—which my eyes tried to give her.

'On God? On *anybody's* God?'

Jenny nodded yes.

'May I explain, Phil?' I asked.

'*Please.*'

'We neither of us believe, Phil. And we won't be hypocrites.'

I think he took it because it came from

me. He might maybe have hit Jenny. But now he was the odd man out, the foreigner. He couldn't look at either of us.

'That's fine,' he said after a very long time. 'Could I just be informed as to who performs the ceremony?'

'We do,' I said.

He looked at his daughter for verification. She nodded. My statement was correct.

After another long silence, he again said, 'That's fine.' And then he inquired of me, inasmuch as I was planning a career in law, whether such a kind of marriage is—what's the word?—legal?

Jenny explained that the ceremony we had in mind would have the college Unitarian chaplain preside ('Ah, chaplain,' murmured Phil) while the man and woman address each other.

'The bride speaks too?' he asked, almost as if this—of all things—might be the coup de grâce.

'Philip,' said his daughter, 'could you imagine any situation in which I would shut up?'

'No, baby,' he replied, working up a tiny smile. 'I guess you would have to talk.'

As we drove back to Cambridge, I asked Jenny how she thought it all went.

'Okay,' she said.

X

Mr William F. Thompson, Associate Dean of the Harvard Law School, could not believe his ears.

'Did I hear you right, Mr Barrett?'

'Yes, sir, Dean Thompson.'

It had not been easy to say the first time. It was no easier repeating it.

'I'll need a scholarship for next year, sir.'

'Really?'

'That's why I'm here, sir. You are in charge of Financial Aid, aren't you, Dean Thompson?'

'Yes, but it's rather curious. Your father—'

'He's no longer involved, sir.'

'I beg your pardon?' Dean Thompson took off his glasses and began to polish them with his tie.

'He and I have had a sort of disagreement.'

The Dean put his glasses back on, and looked at me with that kind of expressionless expression you have to be a dean to master.

'This is very unfortunate, Mr Barrett,' he said. For whom? I wanted to say. This guy was beginning to piss me off.

'Yes, sir,' I said. 'Very unfortunate. But that's why I've come to you, sir. I'm getting married next month. We'll both be working over the summer. Then Jenny—that's my wife—will be teaching in a private school.

That's a living, but it's still not tuition. Your tuition is pretty steep, Dean Thompson.'

'Uh—yes,' he replied. But that's all. Didn't this guy get the drift of my conversation? Why in hell did he think I was there, anyway?

'Dean Thompson, I would like a scholarship.' I said it straight out. A third time. 'I have absolutely zilch in the bank, and I'm already accepted.'

'Ah, yes,' said Mr Thompson, hitting upon the technicality. 'The final date for financial-aid applications is long overdue.'

What would satisfy this bastard? The gory details, maybe? Was it scandal he wanted? What?

'Dean Thompson, when I applied I didn't know this would come up.'

'That's quite right, Mr Barrett, and I must tell you that I really don't think this office should enter into a family quarrel. A rather distressing one, at that.'

'Okay, Dean,' I said, standing up. 'I can see what you're driving at. But I'm still not gonna kiss my father's ass so you can get a Barrett Hall for the Law School.'

As I turned to leave, I heard Dean Thompson mutter, 'That's unfair.'

I couldn't have agreed more.

XI

Jennifer was awarded her degree on Wednesday. All sorts of relatives from Cranston, Fall River—and even an aunt from Cleveland—flocked to Cambridge to attend the ceremony. By prior arrangement, I was not introduced as her fiancé, and Jenny wore no ring: this so that none would be offended (too soon) about missing our wedding.

'Aunt Clara, this is my boyfriend Oliver,' Jenny would say, always adding, '*He* isn't a college graduate.'

There was plenty of rib poking, whispering and even overt speculation, but the relatives could pry no specific information from either of us—or from Phil, who I guess was happy to avoid a discussion of love among the atheists.

On Thursday, I became Jenny's academic equal, receiving my degree from Harvard—like her own, magna cum laude. Moreover, I was Class Marshal, and in this capacity got to lead the graduating seniors to their seats. This meant walking ahead of even the summas, the super-superbrains. I was almost moved to tell these types that my presence as their leader decisively proved my theory that an hour in Dillon Field House is worth two in Widener Library. But I refrained. Let the joy be universal.

I have no idea whether Oliver Barrett III was present. More than seventeen thousand people jam into Harvard Yard on Commencement morning, and I certainly was not scanning the rows with binoculars. Obviously, I had used my allotted parent tickets for Phil and Jenny. Of course, as an alumnus, Old Stonyface could enter and sit with the Class of '26. But then why should he want to? I mean, weren't the banks open?

The wedding was that Sunday. Our reason for excluding Jenny's relatives was out of genuine concern that our omission of the Father, Son and Holy Ghost would make the occasion far too trying for unlapsed Catholics. It was in Phillips Brooks House, an old building in the north of Harvard Yard. Timothy Blauvelt, the college Unitarian chaplain, presided. Naturally, Ray Stratton was there, and I also invited Jeremy Nahum, a good friend from the Exeter days, who had taken Amherst over Harvard. Jenny asked a girl friend from Briggs Hall and—maybe for sentimental reasons— her tall, gawky colleague at the reserve book desk. And of course Phil.

I put Ray Stratton in charge of Phil. I mean, just to keep him as loose as possible. Not that Stratton was all that calm! The pair of them stood there, looking tremendously uncomfortable, each silently reinforcing the other's preconceived notion that this 'do-it-yourself wedding' (as Phil referred to it) was going to be (as Stratton kept predicting) 'an incredible horror show'. Just because Jenny and I were going to address a few words directly to one another! We had actually seen it done earlier that spring when one of Jenny's musical friends, Marya Randall, married a design student named Eric Levenson. It was a very beautiful thing, and really sold us on the idea.

'Are you two ready?' asked Mr Blauvelt.

'Yes,' I said for both of us.

'Friends,' said Mr Blauvelt to the others, 'we are here to witness the union of two lives in marriage. Let us listen to the words they have chosen to read on this sacred occasion.'

The bride first. Jenny stood facing me and recited the poem she had selected. It was very moving, perhaps especially to me, because it was a sonnet by Elizabeth Barrett:

When our two souls stand up erect and
    strong,
Face to face, silent, drawing nigh and
    nigher,
Until the lengthening wings break into fire
    . . .

From the corner of my eye I saw Phil Cavilleri, pale, slack-jawed, eyes wide with amazement and adoration combined. We listened to Jenny finish the sonnet, which was in its way a kind of prayer for

> A place to stand and love in for a day,
> With darkness and the death hour rounding
>   it.

Then it was my turn. It had been hard finding a piece of poetry I could read without blushing. I mean, I couldn't stand there and recite lace-doily phrases. I couldn't. But a section of Walt Whitman's Song of the Open Road, though kind of brief, said it all for me:

> . . . I give you my hand!
> I give you my love more precious than money,
> I give you myself before preaching or law;
> Will you give me yourself? will you come
>   travel with me?

Shall we stick by each other as long as we
    live?

I finished, and there was a wonderful hush
in the room. Then Ray Stratton handed me
the ring, and Jenny and I—ourselves—recited
the marriage vows, taking each other, from
that day forward, to love and cherish, till
death do us part.

By the authority vested in him by the
Commonwealth of Massachusetts, Mr Timothy
Blauvelt pronounced us man and wife.

* * *

Upon reflection, our 'post-game party' (as
Stratton referred to it) was pretentiously
unpretentious. Jenny and I had absolutely
rejected the champagne route, and since there
were so few of us we could all fit into one
booth, we went to drink beer at Cronin's. As

I recall, Jim Cronin himself set us up with a round, as a tribute to 'the greatest Harvard hockey player since the Cleary brothers.'

'Like hell,' argued Phil Cavilleri, pounding his fist on the table. 'He's better than all the Clearys put together.' Philip's meaning, I believe (he had never seen a Harvard hockey game), was that however well Bobby or Billy Cleary might have skated, neither got to marry his lovely daughter. I mean, we were all smashed, and it was just an excuse for getting more so.

I let Phil pick up the tab, a decision which later evoked one of Jenny's rare compliments about my intuition ('You'll be a human being yet, Preppie'). It got a little hairy at the end when we drove him to the bus, however. I mean the wet-eyes bit. His, Jenny's, maybe mine too; I don't remember anything except that the moment was liquid.

Anyway, after all sorts of blessings, he got onto the bus and we waited and waved until it drove out of sight. It was then that the awesome truth started to get to me.

'Jenny, we're legally married!'

'Yeah, now I can be a bitch.'

XII

If a single word can describe our daily life during those first three years, it is 'scrounge'. Every waking moment we were concentrating on how the hell we would be able to scrape up enough dough to do whatever it was we had to do. Usually it was just break even. And there's nothing romantic about it, either. Remember the famous stanza in Omar Khayyám? You know, the book of verses underneath the bough, the loaf of bread, the jug of wine and so forth? Substitute *Scott on Trusts* for that book of verses and see how this poetic vision stacks up against my idyllic existence. Ah, paradise? No, bullshit. All I'd think about is how much that book was (could we get it second-hand?) and where, if anywhere, we might be able to charge that bread and wine. And then how we might ultimately scrounge up the dough to pay off our debts.

Life changes. Even the simplest decision must be scrutinized by the ever vigilant budget committee of your mind.

'Hey, Oliver, let's go see Becket tonight.'

'Listen, it's three bucks.'

'What do you mean?'

'I mean a buck fifty for you and a buck fifty for me.'

'Does that mean yes or no?'

'Neither. It just means three bucks.'

Our honeymoon was spent on a yacht and with twenty-one children. That is, I sailed a thirty-six-foot Rhodes from seven in the morning till whenever my passengers had enough, and Jenny was a children's counselor. It was a place called the Pequod Boat Club in Dennis Port (not far from Hyannis), an establishment that included a large hotel, a marina and several dozen houses for rent. In one of the tinier bungalows, I have nailed an imaginary plaque: 'Oliver and Jenny slept here—when they weren't making love.' I think it's a tribute to us both that after a long day of being kind to our customers, for we were largely dependent on their tips for our income, Jenny and I were nonetheless kind to each other. I simply say 'kind,' because I lack the vocabulary to describe what loving and being loved by Jennifer Cavilleri is like. Sorry, I mean Jennifer Barrett.

Before leaving for the Cape, we found a

cheap apartment in North Cambridge. I called it North Cambridge, although the address was technically in the town of Somerville and the house was, as Jenny described it, 'in the state of disrepair.' It had originally been a two-family structure, now converted into four apartments, overpriced even at its 'cheap' rental. But what the hell can graduate students do? It's a seller's market.

'Hey, Ol, why do you think the fire department hasn't condemned the joint?' Jenny asked.

'They're probably afraid to walk inside,' I said.

'So am I.'

'You weren't in June,' I said.

(This dialogue was taking place upon our reentry in September.)

'I wasn't married then. Speaking as a married woman, I consider this place to be unsafe at any speed.'

'What do you intend to do about it?'

'Speak to my husband,' she replied. 'He'll take care of it.'

'Hey, I'm your husband,' I said.

'Really? Prove it.'

'How?' I asked, inwardly thinking, Oh no, in the street?

'Carry me over the threshold,' she said.

'You don't believe in that nonsense, do you?'

'Carry me, and I'll decide after.'

Okay. I scooped her in my arms and hauled her up five steps onto the porch.

'Why'd you stop?' she asked.

'Isn't this the threshold?'

'Negative, negative,' she said.

'I see our name by the bell.'

'This is not the official goddamn threshold. Upstairs, you turkey!'

It was twenty-four steps up to our 'official' homestead, and I had to pause about halfway to catch my breath.

'Why are you so heavy?' I asked her.

'Did you ever think I might be pregnant?' she answered.

This didn't make it easier for me to catch my breath.

'Are you?' I could finally say.

'Hah! Scared you, didn't I?'

'Nah.'

'Don't bullshit me, Preppie.'

'Yeah. For a second there, I clutched.'

I carried her the rest of the way.

This is among the precious few moments I can recall in which the verb 'scrounge' has no relevance whatever.

My illustrious name enabled us to establish a charge account at a grocery store which would otherwise have denied credit to students. And yet it worked to our disadvantage at a place I would least have expected: the Shady Lane School, where Jenny was to teach.

'Of course, Shady Lane isn't able to match the public school salaries,' Miss Anne Miller Whitman, the principal, told my wife, adding something to the effect that Barretts wouldn't be concerned with 'that aspect' anyway. Jenny tried to dispel her illusions, but all she could get in addition to the already offered thirty-five hundred for the year was about two minutes of 'ho ho ho's. Miss Whitman thought Jenny was being so witty in her remarks about Barretts having to pay the rent just like other people.

When Jenny recounted all this to me, I made a few imaginative suggestions about what Miss Whitman could do with her—ho ho ho—thirty-five hundred. But then Jenny asked if I would like to drop out of law school and support her while she took the education credits needed to teach in a public school. I gave the whole situation a big think for about two seconds and reached an accurate and succinct conclusion:

'Shit.'

'That's pretty eloquent,' said my wife.

'What am I supposed to say, Jenny—"ho ho ho"?'

'No. Just learn to like spaghetti.'

I did. I learned to like spaghetti, and Jenny learned every conceivable recipe to make pasta seem like something else. What with our summer earnings, her salary, the income anticipated from my planned night work in the post office during Christmas rush, we were doing okay. I mean, there were a lot of movies we didn't see (and concerts she didn't go to), but we were making ends meet.

Of course, about all we were meeting were ends. I mean, socially both our lives changed drastically. We were still in Cambridge, and theoretically Jenny could have stayed with all her music groups. But there wasn't time. She came home from Shady Lane exhausted, and there was dinner yet to cook (eating out was beyond the realm of maximum feasibility). Meanwhile my own friends were considerate enough to let us alone. I mean, they didn't invite us so we wouldn't have to invite them, if you know what I mean.

We even skipped the football games.

As a member of the Varsity Club, I was entitled to seats in their terrific section on the fifty-yard line. But it was six bucks a ticket, which is twelve bucks.

'It's not,' argued Jenny, 'it's six bucks. You can go without me. I don't know a thing about football except people shout "Hit 'em again," which is what you adore, which is why I want you to goddamn go!'

'The case is closed,' I would reply, being after all the husband and head of household. 'Besides, I can use the time to study.' Still, I would spend Saturday afternoons with a transistor at my ear, listening to the roar of the fans, who, though geographically but a mile away, were now in another world.

I used my Varsity Club privileges to get Yale game seats for Robbie Wald, a Law School classmate. When Robbie left our apartment, effusively grateful, Jenny asked if I wouldn't tell her again just who got to sit in the V. Club section, and I once more explained that it was for those who, regardless of age or size or social rank, had nobly served fair Harvard on the playing fields.

'On the water too?' she asked.

'Jocks are jocks,' I answered, 'dry or wet.'

'Except you, Oliver,' she said. 'You're frozen.'

I let the subject drop, assuming that this was simply Jennifer's usual flip repartee, not wanting to think there had been any more to her question concerning the athletic traditions of Harvard University. Such as perhaps the subtle suggestion that although

Soldiers Field holds 45,000 people, all former athletes would be seated in that one terrific section. All. Old and young. Wet, dry—and even frozen. And was it merely six dollars that kept me away from the stadium those Saturday afternoons?

No; if she had something else in mind, I would rather not discuss it.

XIII

Mr and Mrs Oliver Barrett III
request the pleasure of your company
at a dinner in celebration of
Mr Barrett's sixtieth birthday
Saturday, the sixth of March
at seven o'clock
Dover House, Ipswich, Massachusetts

R.s.v.p.

'Well?' asked Jennifer.

'Do you even have to ask?' I replied. I was in the midst of abstracting *The State v. Percival*, a crucial precedent in criminal law. Jenny was sort of waving the invitation to bug me.

'I think it's about time, Oliver,' she said.

'For what?'

'For you know very well what,' she answered. 'Does he have to crawl here on his hands and knees?'

I kept working as she worked me over.

'Ollie—he's reaching out to you!'

'Bullshit, Jenny. My mother addressed the envelope.'

'I thought you said you didn't look at it!' she sort of yelled.

Okay, so I did glance at it earlier. Maybe it had slipped my mind. I was, after all, in the midst of abstracting *The State v. Percival*, and in the virtual shadow of exams. The point was she should have stopped haranguing me.

'Ollie, think,' she said, her tone kind of pleading now. 'Sixty goddamn years old. Nothing says he'll still be around when *you're* finally ready for the reconciliation.'

I informed Jenny in the simplest possible terms that there would never be a reconciliation and would she please let me continue my studying. She sat down quietly, squeezing herself onto a corner of the hassock where I had my feet. Although she didn't make a sound, I quickly became aware that she was looking at me very hard. I glanced up.

'Someday,' she said, 'when you're being bugged by Oliver V—'

'He won't be called *Oliver*, be sure of that!' I snapped at her. She didn't raise her voice, though she usually did when I did.

'Lissen, Ol, even if we name him Bozo the Clown, that kid's still gonna resent you 'cause you were a big Harvard jock. And by the time he's a freshman, you'll probably be in the Supreme Court!'

I told her that our son would definitely not resent me. She then inquired how I could be so certain of that. I couldn't produce evidence. I mean, I simply knew our son would not resent me, I couldn't *say* precisely why. As an absolute non sequitur, Jenny then remarked:

'Your father loves you too, Oliver. He loves you just the way you'll love Bozo. But you Barretts are so damn proud and competitive, you'll go through life thinking you hate each other.'

'If it weren't for you,' I said facetiously.

'Yes,' she said.

'The case is closed,' I said, being after all the husband and head of household. My eyes returned to *The State v. Percival* and Jenny got up. But then she remembered:

'There's still the matter of the RSVP.'

I allowed that a Radcliffe music major

could probably compose a nice little negative RSVP without professional guidance.

'Lissen, Oliver,' she said, 'I've probably lied or cheated in my life. But I've never deliberately hurt anyone. I don't think I could.'

Really, at that moment she was only hurting me, so I asked her politely to handle the RSVP in whatever manner she wished, as long as the essence of the message was that we wouldn't show unless hell froze over. I returned once again to *The State v. Percival*.

'What's the number?' I heard her say very softly. She was at the telephone.

'Can't you just write a note?'

'In a minute I'll lose my nerve. What's the number?'

I told her and was instantaneously immersed in Percival's appeal to the Supreme Court. I was not listening to Jenny. That is, I tried not to. She was in the same room, after all.

'Oh—good evening, sir,' I heard her say. Did the Sonovabitch answer the phone? Wasn't he in Washington during the week? That's what a recent profile in *The New York Times* said. Goddamn journalism is going downhill nowadays.

How long does it take to say no?

Somehow Jennifer had already taken more time than one would think necessary to pronounce this simple syllable.

'Ollie?'

She had her hand over the mouthpiece.

'Ollie, does it *have* to be negative?'

The nod of my head indicated that it had to be, the wave of my hand indicated that she should hurry the hell up.

'I'm terribly sorry,' she said into the phone. 'I mean, *we're* terribly sorry, sir . . .'

We're! Did she have to involve me in this? And why can't she get to the point and hang up?

'Oliver!'

She had her hand on the mouthpiece again and was talking very loud.

'He's wounded, Oliver! Can you just sit there and let your father bleed?'

Had she not been in such an emotional state, I could have explained once again that stones do not bleed, that she should not project her Italian-Mediterranean misconceptions about parents onto the craggy heights of Mount Rushmore. But she was very upset. And it was upsetting me too.

'Oliver,' she pleaded, 'could you just say a word?'

To *him*? She must be going out of her mind!

'I mean, like just maybe "hello"?'

She was offering the phone to me. And trying not to cry.

'I will never talk to him. Ever,' I said with perfect calm.

And now she was crying. Nothing audible, but tears pouring down her face. And then she—she begged.

'For *me*, Oliver. I've never asked you for anything. Please.'

Three of us. Three of us just standing (I somehow imagined my father being there as well) waiting for something. What? For me?

I couldn't do it.

Didn't Jenny understand she was asking the impossible? That I would have done absolutely anything else? As I looked at the floor, shaking my head in adamant refusal and extreme discomfort, Jenny addressed me with a kind of whispered fury I had never heard from her:

'You are a heartless bastard,' she said. And then she ended the telephone conversation with my father, saying:

'Mr Barrett, Oliver does want you to know that in his own special way . . .'

She paused for breath. She had been sobbing, so it wasn't easy. I was much too astonished to do anything but await the end of my alleged 'message.'

'Oliver loves you very much,' she said, and hung up very quickly.

There is no rational explanation for my actions in the next split second. I plead temporary insanity. Correction: I plead nothing. I must never be forgiven for what I did.

I ripped the phone from her hand, then from the socket—and hurled it across the room.

'God damn you, Jenny! Why don't you get the hell out of my life!'

I stood still, panting like the animal I had suddenly become. Jesus Christ! What the hell had happened to me? I turned to look at Jen.

But she was gone.

I mean absolutely gone, because I didn't

even hear footsteps on the stairs. Christ, she must have dashed out the instant I grabbed the phone. Even her coat and scarf were still there. The pain of not knowing what to do was exceeded only by that of knowing what I had done.

I searched everywhere.

In the Law School library, I prowled the rows of grinding students, looking and looking. Up and back, at least half a dozen times. Though I didn't utter a sound, I knew my glance was so intense, my face so fierce, I was disturbing the whole fucking place. Who cares?

But Jenny wasn't there.

Then all through Harkness Commons, the lounge, the cafeteria. Then a wild sprint to look around Agassiz Hall at Radcliffe. Not there, either. I was running everywhere now, my legs trying to catch up with the pace of my heart.

Paine Hall? (Ironic goddamn name!) Downstairs are piano practice rooms. I know Jenny. When she's angry, she pounds the fucking keyboard. Right? But how about when she's scared to death?

It's crazy walking down the corridor, practice rooms on either side. The sounds of Mozart and Bartók, Bach and Brahms filter out from the doors and blend into this weird infernal sound.

Jenny's got to be here!

Instinct made me stop at a door where I heard the pounding (angry?) sound of a Chopin prelude. I paused for a second. The playing was lousy—stops and starts and many mistakes. At one pause I heard a girl's voice mutter, 'Shit!' It had to be Jenny. I flung open the door.

A Radcliffe girl was at the piano. She looked up. An ugly, big-shouldered hippie Radcliffe girl, annoyed at my invasion.

'What's the scene, man?' she asked.

'Bad, bad,' I replied, and closed the door again.

Then I tried Harvard Square. The Café Pamplona, Tommy's Arcade, even Hayes Bick—lots of artistic types go there. *Nothing*.

Where would Jenny have gone?

By now the subway was closed, but if she had gone straight to the Square she could have caught a train to Boston. To the bus terminal.

It was almost 1 a.m. as I deposited a quarter and two dimes in the slot. I was in one of the booths by the kiosk in Harvard Square.

'Hello, Phil?'

'Hey . . .' he said sleepily. 'Who's this?'

'It's me—Oliver.'

'Oliver!' He sounded scared. 'Is Jenny hurt?' he asked quickly. If he was asking me, did that mean she wasn't with him?

'Uh—no, Phil, no.'

'Thank Christ. How are you, Oliver?'

Once assured of his daughter's safety, he was casual and friendly. As if he had not been aroused from the depths of slumber.

'Fine, Phil, I'm great. Fine. Say, Phil, what do you hear from Jenny?'

'Not enough, goddammit,' he answered in a strangely calm voice.

'What do you mean, Phil?'

'Christ, she should call more often, goddammit. I'm not a stranger, you know.'

If you can be relieved and panicked at the same time, that's what I was.

'Is she there with you?' he asked me.

'Huh?'

'Put Jenny on; I'll yell at her myself.'

'I can't, Phil.'

'Oh, is she asleep? If she's asleep, don't disturb her.'

'Yeah,' I said.

'Listen, you bastard,' he said.

'Yes, sir?'

'How goddamn far is Cranston that you can't come down on a Sunday afternoon? Huh? Or I can come up, Oliver.'

'Uh—no, Phil. We'll come down.'

'When?'

'Some Sunday.'

'Don't give me that "some" crap. A loyal child doesn't say "some", he says "this". This Sunday, Oliver.'

'Yes, sir. This Sunday.'

'Four o'clock. But drive carefully. Right?'

'Right.'

'And next time call collect, goddammit.'

He hung up.

I just stood there, lost on that island in the dark of Harvard Square, not knowing where to go or what to do next. A colored guy approached me and inquired if I was in need of a fix. I kind of absently replied, 'No, thank you, sir.'

I wasn't running now. I mean, what was the rush to return to the empty house? It was very late and I was numb—more with fright than with the cold (although it wasn't warm, believe me). From several yards off, I thought I saw someone sitting on the top of the steps. This had to be my eyes playing tricks, because the figure was motionless.

But it was Jenny.

She was sitting on the top step.

I was too tired to panic, too relieved to speak. Inwardly I hoped she had some blunt instrument with which to hit me.

'Jen?'

'Ollie?'

We both spoke so quietly, it was impossible to take an emotional reading.

'I forgot my key,' Jenny said.

I stood there at the bottom of the steps, afraid to ask how long she had been sitting, knowing only that I had wronged her terribly.

'Jenny, I'm sorry—'

'Stop!' She cut off my apology, then said very quietly, 'Love means not ever having to say you're sorry.'

I climbed up the stairs to where she was sitting.

'I'd like to go to sleep. Okay?' she said.

'Okay.'

We walked up to our apartment. As we undressed, she looked at me reassuringly.

'I meant what I said, Oliver.'

And that was all.

XIV

It was July when the letter came.

It had been forwarded from Cambridge to Dennis Port, so I guess I got the news a day or so late. I charged over to where Jenny was supervising her children in a game of kickball (or something); and said in my best Bogart tones:

'Let's go.'

'Huh?'

'Let's go,' I repeated with such authority that she actually started to follow me as I walked off the field.

'Let's go,' I repeated, and with such obvious authority that she began to follow me as I walked toward the water.

'What's going on, Oliver? Wouldja tell me, please, for God sake?'

I continued to stride powerfully onto the dock.

'Onto the boat, Jennifer,' I ordered, pointing to it with the very hand that held the letter, which she didn't even notice.

'Oliver, I have children to take care of,' she protested, even while stepping obediently on board.

'Goddammit, Oliver, will you explain what's going on?'

We were now a few hundred yards from shore.

'I have something to tell you,' I said.

'Couldn't you have told it on dry land?' she yelled.

'No, goddammit,' I yelled back (we were neither of us angry, but there was lots of wind, and we had to shout to be heard).

'I wanted to be alone with you. Look what I have.'

I waved the envelope at her. She immediately recognized the letterhead.

'Hey—Harvard Law School! Have you been kicked out?'

'Guess again, you optimistic bitch,' I yelled.

'You were first in the class!' she guessed.

I was now almost ashamed to tell her.

'Not quite. Third.'

'Oh,' she said. 'Only third?'

'Listen—that still means I make the goddamn *Law Review*,' I shouted.

She just sat there with an absolute no-expression expression.

'Christ, Jenny,' I kind of whined, 'say something?'

'Not until I meet numbers one and two,' she said.

I looked at her, hoping she would break into the smile I knew she was suppressing.

'C'mon, Jenny!' I pleaded.

'I'm leaving. Good-bye,' she said, and jumped immediately into the water. I dove right in after her and the next thing I knew we were both hanging on to the side of the boat and giggling.

'Hey,' I said in one of my wittier observations, 'you went overboard for me.'

'Don't be too cocky,' she replied. 'Third is still only third.'

'Hey, listen, you bitch,' I said.

'What, you bastard?' she replied.

'I owe you a helluva lot,' I said sincerely.

'Not true, you bastard, not true,' she answered.

'Not true?' I inquired, somewhat surprised.

'You owe me everything,' she said.

That night we blew twenty-three bucks on a lobster dinner at a fancy place in Yarmouth. Jenny was still reserving judgment until she could check out the two gentlemen who had, as she put it, 'defeated me.'

Stupid as it sounds, I was so in love with her that the moment we got back to Cambridge, I rushed to find out who the first two guys were. I was relieved to discover that the top man, Erwin Blasband, City College '64, was bookish, bespectacled, nonathletic and not her type, and the number-two man was Bella Landau, Bryn Mawr '64, a girl. This was all to the good, especially since Bella Landau was rather cool looking (as lady law students go), and I could twit Jenny a bit with 'details' of what went on in those late-night hours at Gannett House, the *Law Review* building. And Jesus, there were late nights. It was not unusual for me to come home at two or three in the morning. I mean, six courses, plus editing the *Law Review*, plus the fact that I actually authored an article in one of the issues ('Legal Assistance for the Urban Poor: A Study of Boston's Roxbury District' by Oliver Barrett IV, HLR, March, 1966, pp. 861–908).

'A good piece. A really good piece.'

That's all Joel Fleishman, the senior editor, could repeat again and again. Frankly, I had expected a more articulate compliment from the guy who would next year clerk for Justice Douglas, but that's all he kept saying as he checked over my final draft. Christ, Jenny had told me it was 'incisive, intelligent and really well written.' Couldn't Fleishman match that?

'Fleishman called it a good piece, Jen.'

'Jesus, did I wait up so late just to hear

that?' she said. 'Didn't he comment on your research, or your style, or *anything*?'

'No, Jen. He just called it "good".'

'Then what took you all this long?'

I gave her a little wink.

'I had some stuff to go over with Bella Landau,' I said.

'Oh?' she said.

I couldn't read the tone.

'Are you jealous?' I asked straight out.

'No; I've got much better legs,' she said.

'Can you write a brief?'

'Can she make lasagna?'

'Yes,' I answered. 'Matter of fact, she brought some over to Gannett House tonight. Everybody said they were as good as your legs.'

Jenny nodded, 'I'll bet.'

'What do you say to that?' I said.

'Does Bella Landau pay your rent?' she asked.

'Damn,' I replied, 'why can't I ever quit when I'm ahead?'

'Because, Preppie,' said my loving wife, 'you never are.'

XV

We finished in that order.

I mean, Erwin, Bella and myself were the top three in the Law School graduating class. The time for triumph was at hand. Job interviews. Offers. Pleas. Snow jobs. Everywhere I turned somebody seemed to be waving a flag that read: 'Work for us, Barrett!'

But I followed only the green flags. I mean, I wasn't totally crass, but I eliminated the prestige alternatives, like clerking for a judge, and the public service alternatives, like Department of Justice, in favor of a lucrative job that would get the dirty word 'scrounge' out of our goddamn vocabulary.

Third though I was, I enjoyed one inestimable advantage in competing for the best legal spots. I was the only guy in the top ten who wasn't Jewish. (And anyone who says it doesn't matter is full of it.) Christ, there are dozens of firms who will kiss the ass of a WASP who can merely pass the bar. Consider the case of yours truly: *Law Review*, All-Ivy, Harvard and you know what else. Hordes of people were fighting to get my name and numeral onto their stationery. I felt like a bonus baby—and I loved every minute of it.

There was one especially intriguing offer from a firm in Los Angeles. The recruiter, Mr—(why risk a lawsuit?), kept telling me:

'Barrett baby, in our territory we get it all the time. Day and night. I mean, we can even have it sent up to the office!'

Not that we were interested in California, but I'd still like to know precisely what Mr— was discussing. Jenny and I came up with some pretty wild possibilities, but for L.A. they probably weren't wild enough. (I finally had to get Mr—off my back by telling him that I really didn't care for 'it' at all. He was crestfallen.)

Actually, we had made up our minds to stay on the East Coast. As it turned out, we still had dozens of fantastic offers from Boston, New York and Washington. Jenny at one time thought D.C. might be good ('You could check out the White House, Ol'), but I leaned toward New York. And so, with my wife's blessing, I finally said yes to the firm of Jonas and Marsh, a prestigious office (Marsh was a former Attorney General) that was very civil-liberties oriented ('You can do good *and* make good at once,' said Jenny). Also, they really snowed me. I mean, old man Jonas came up to Boston, took us to dinner at Pier Four and sent Jenny flowers the next day.

Jenny went around for a week sort of singing a jingle that went 'Jonas, Marsh and Barrett.' I told her not so fast and she told me to go screw because I was probably singing the same tune in my head. I don't have to tell you she was right.

Allow me to mention, however, that Jonas and Marsh paid Oliver Barrett IV $11,800, the absolute highest salary received by any member of our graduating class.

So you see I was only third *academically*.

XVI

CHANGE OF ADDRESS
From July 1, 1967
    Mr and Mrs Oliver Barrett IV
    263 East 63rd Street
    New York, N.Y. 10021

'It's so nouveau riche,' complained Jenny.
  'But we are nouveau riche,' I insisted.

What was adding to my overall feeling of euphoric triumph was the fact that the monthly rate for my car was damn near as much as we had paid for our entire apartment in Cambridge! Jonas and Marsh was an easy ten-minute walk (or strut—I preferred the latter gait), and so were the fancy shops like Bonwit's and so forth where I insisted that my wife, the bitch, immediately open accounts and start spending.

'*Why, Oliver?*'

'*Because, goddammit, Jenny, I want to be taken advantage of!*'

I joined the Harvard Club of New York, proposed by Raymond Stratton '64, newly returned to civilian life after having actually shot at some Vietcong ('I'm not positive it was VC, actually. I heard noises, so I opened fire at the bushes'). Ray and I played squash at least three times a week, and I made a mental note, giving myself three years to become

Club champion. Whether it was merely because I had resurfaced in Harvard territory, or because word of my Law School successes had gotten around (I didn't brag about the salary, honest), my 'friends' discovered me once more. We had moved in at the height of the summer (I had to take a cram course for the New York bar exam), and the first invitations were for weekends.

'Fuck 'em, Oliver. I don't want to waste two days bullshitting with a bunch of vapid preppies.'

'Okay, Jen, but what should I *tell* them?'

'Just say I'm pregnant, Oliver.'

'Are you?' I asked.

'No, but if we stay home this weekend I might be.'

We had a name already picked out. I mean, I had, and I think I got Jenny to agree finally.

'Hey—you won't laugh?' I said to her,

when first broaching the subject. She was in the kitchen at the time (a yellow color-keyed thing that even included a dishwasher).

'What?' she asked, still slicing tomatoes.

'I've really grown fond of the name Bozo,' I said.

'You mean seriously?' she asked.

'Yeah. I honestly dig it.'

'You would name our child Bozo?' she asked again.

'Yes. Really. Honestly, Jen, it's the name of a super-jock.'

'Bozo Barrett.' She tried it on for size.

'Christ, he'll be an incredible bruiser,' I continued, convincing myself further with each word I spoke. '"Bozo Barrett, Harvard's huge All-Ivy tackle."'

'Yeah—but, Oliver,' she asked, 'suppose—just suppose—the kid's not coordinated?'

'Impossible, Jen, the genes are too good. Truly.' I meant it sincerely. This whole Bozo business had gotten to be a frequent daydream of mine as I strutted to work.

I pursued the matter at dinner. We had bought great Danish china.

'Bozo will be a very well-coordinated bruiser,' I told Jenny. 'In fact, if he has your hands, we can put him in the backfield.'

She was just smirking at me, searching no doubt for some sneaky put-down to disrupt my idyllic vision. But lacking a truly devastating remark, she merely cut the cake and gave me a piece. And she was still hearing me out.

'Think of it, Jenny,' I continued, even with my mouth full, 'two hundred and forty pounds of bruising finesse.'

'Two hundred and forty pounds?' she said. 'There's nothing in our genes that says two hundred and forty pounds, Oliver.'

'We'll feed him up, Jen. Hi-Proteen, Nutrament, the whole diet-supplement bit.'

'Oh, yeah? Suppose he won't eat, Oliver?'

'He'll eat, goddammit,' I said, getting slightly pissed off already at the kid who would soon be sitting at our table not cooperating with my plans for his athletic triumphs. 'He'll eat or I'll break his face.'

At which point Jenny looked me straight in the eye and smiled.

'Not if he weighs two forty, you won't.'

'Oh,' I replied, momentarily set back, then quickly realized, 'But he won't be two forty right away!'

'Yeah, yeah,' said Jenny, now shaking an admonitory spoon at me, 'but when he is, Preppie, start running!' And she laughed like hell.

It's really comic, but while she was laughing I had this vision of a two-hundred-and-forty-pound kid in a diaper chasing after me in Central Park, shouting, 'You be nicer to my mother, Preppie!' Christ, hopefully Jenny would keep Bozo from destroying me.

XVII

It is not all that easy to make a baby.

I mean, there is a certain irony involved when guys who spend the first years of their sex lives preoccupied with *not* getting girls pregnant (and when I first started, condoms were still in) then reverse their thinking and become obsessed with conception and not its contra.

Yes, it can become an obsession. And it can divest the most glorious aspect of a happy married life of its naturalness and spontaneity. I mean, to program your thinking (unfortunate verb, 'program'; it suggests a machine)—to program your thinking about the act of love in accordance with rules, calendars, *strategy* ('Wouldn't it be better tomorrow morning, Ol?') can be a source of discomfort, disgust and ultimately terror.

For when you see that your layman's knowledge and (you assume) normal healthy efforts are not succeeding in the matter of increase-and-multiply, it can bring the most awful thoughts to your mind.

'I'm sure you understand, Oliver, that "sterility" would have nothing to do with "virility".' Thus said Dr Mortimer Sheppard to me during the first conversation, when Jenny and I had finally decided we needed expert consultation.

'He understands, doctor,' said Jenny for me, knowing without my ever having mentioned it that the notion of being sterile—of possibly being sterile—was devastating to me. Didn't her voice even suggest that she hoped, if an insufficiency were to be discovered, it would be her own?

But the doctor had merely been spelling it all out for us, telling us the worst, before going on to say that there was still a great possibility that both of us were okay, and that we might soon be proud parents. But of course we would both undergo a battery of tests. Complete physicals. The works. (I don't want to repeat the unpleasant specifics of this kind of thorough investigation.)

We went through the tests on a Monday, Jenny during the day, I after work (I was fantastically immersed in the legal world). Dr Sheppard called Jenny in again that Friday, explaining that his nurse had screwed up and he needed to check a few things again. When Jenny told me of the revisit, I began to suspect that perhaps he had found the ... insufficiency with her. I think she suspected the same. The nurse-screwing-up alibi is pretty trite.

When Dr Sheppard called me at Jonas and Marsh, I was almost certain. Would I please drop by his office on the way home? When I heard this was not to be a three-way conversation ('I spoke to Mrs Barrett earlier today'), my suspicions were confirmed. Jenny could not have children. Although, let's not phrase it in the absolute, Oliver; remember Sheppard mentioned there were things like corrective surgery and so forth. But I couldn't concentrate at all, and it was foolish to wait it out till five o'clock. I called Sheppard back and asked if he could see me in the early afternoon. He said okay.

'Do you know whose fault it is?' I asked, not mincing any words.

'I really wouldn't say "fault," Oliver,' he replied.

'Well, okay, do you know which of us is *malfunctioning*?'

'Yes. Jenny.'

I had been more or less prepared for this, but the finality with which the doctor pronounced it still threw me. He wasn't saying anything more, so I assumed he wanted a statement of some sort from me.

'Okay, so we'll adopt kids. I mean, the important thing is that we love each other, right?'

And then he told me.

'Oliver, the problem is more serious than that. Jenny is very sick.'

'Would you define "very sick", please?'

'She's dying.'

'That's impossible,' I said.

And I waited for the doctor to tell me that it was all a grim joke.

'She is, Oliver,' he said. 'I'm very sorry to have to tell you this.'

I insisted that he had made some mistake— perhaps that idiot nurse of his had screwed up again and given him the wrong X rays or something. He replied with as much compassion as he could that Jenny's blood test had been repeated three times. There was absolutely no question about the diagnosis. He would of course have to refer us—me— Jenny to a hematologist. In fact, he could suggest—

I waved my hand to cut him off. I wanted silence for a minute. Just silence to let it all sink in. Then a thought occurred to me.

'What did you tell Jenny, doctor?'

'That you were both all right.'

'She bought it?'

'I think so.'

'When do we have to tell her?'

'At this point, it's up to you.'

Up to me! Christ, at this point I didn't feel up to breathing.

The doctor explained that what therapy they had for Jenny's form of leukemia was merely palliative—it could relieve, it might retard, but it could not reverse. So at this point it was up to me. They could withhold therapy for a while.

But at that moment all I really could think of was how obscene the whole fucking thing was.

'She's only twenty-four!' I told the doctor, shouting, I think. He nodded, very patiently, knowing full well Jenny's age, but also understanding what agony this was for me. Finally I realized that I couldn't just sit in this man's office forever. So I asked him what to do. I mean, what I should do. He told me to act as normal as possible for as long as possible. I thanked him and left.

Normal! *Normal*!

XVIII

I began to think about God.

I mean, the notion of a Supreme Being existing somewhere began to creep into my private thoughts. Not because I wanted to strike Him on the face, to punch Him out for what He was about to do to me—to Jenny, that is. No, the kind of religious thoughts I had were just the opposite. Like when I woke up in the morning and Jenny was there. Still there. I'm sorry, embarrassed even, but I hoped there was a God I could say thank you to. Thank you for letting me wake up and see Jennifer.

I was trying like hell to act normal, so of course I let her make breakfast and so forth.

'Seing Stratton today?' she asked, as I was having a second bowl of Special K.

'Who?' I asked.

'Raymond Stratton '64,' she said, 'your best friend. Your roommate before me.'

'Yeah. We were supposed to play squash. I think I'll cancel it.'

'Bullshit.'

'What, Jen?'

'Don't go canceling squash games, Preppie. I don't want a flabby husband, dammit!'

'Okay,' I said, 'but let's have dinner downtown.'

'Why?' she asked.

'What do you mean, "why"?' I yelled, trying to work up my normal mock anger. 'Can't I take my goddamn wife to dinner if I want to?'

'Who is she, Barrett? What's her name?' Jenny asked.

'What?'

'Listen,' she explained. 'When you have to take your wife to dinner on a weekday, you must be screwing someone!'

'Jennifer!' I bellowed, now honestly hurt. 'I will not have that kind of talk at my breakfast table!'

'Then get your ass home to my dinner table. Okay?'

'Okay.'

And I told this God, whoever and wherever He might be, that I would gladly settle for the status quo. I don't mind the agony, sir, I don't mind knowing as long as Jenny doesn't know. Did you hear me, Lord, sir? You can name the price.

* * *

'Oliver?'

'Yes, Mr Jonas?'

He had called me into his office.

'Are you familiar with the Beck affair?' he asked.

Of course I was. Robert L. Beck, photographer for *Life* magazine, had the shit kicked out of him by the Chicago police, while trying to photograph a riot. Jonas considered this one of the key cases for the firm.

'I know the cops punched him out, sir,' I told Jonas, lightheartedly (hah!).

'I'd like you to handle it, Oliver,' he said.

'Myself?' I asked.

'You can take along one of the younger men,' he replied.

Younger men? I was the youngest guy in the office. But I read his message: Oliver, despite your chronological age, you are already one of the elders of this office. One of *us*, Oliver.

'Thank you, sir,' I said.

'How soon can you leave for Chicago?' he asked.

I had resolved to tell nobody, to shoulder the entire burden myself. So I gave old man Jonas some bullshit, I don't even remember exactly what, about how I didn't feel I could leave New York at this time, sir. And I hoped he would understand. But I know he was disappointed at my reaction to what was obviously a very significant gesture. Oh, Christ, Mr Jonas, when you find out the real reason!

* * *

Paradox: Oliver Barrett IV leaving the office earlier, yet walking homeward more slowly. How can you explain that?

I had gotten into the habit of window shopping on Fifth Avenue, looking at the wonderful and silly extravagant things I would have bought Jennifer had I not wanted to keep up that fiction of . . . normal.

Sure, I was afraid to go home. Because now, several weeks after I had first learned the true facts, she was beginning to lose weight. I mean, just a little and she herself probably didn't notice. But I, who knew, noticed.

I would window shop the airlines: Brazil, the Caribbean, Hawaii ('Get away from it all—fly into the sunshine!') and so forth. On this particular afternoon, TWA was pushing Europe in the off season: London for shoppers, Paris for lovers . . .

'*What about my scholarship? What about Paris, which I've never seen in my whole goddam life?*'

'*What about our marriage?*'

'*Who said anything about marriage?*'

'*Me. I'm saying it now.*'

'*You want to marry me?*'

'*Yes.*'

'*Why?*'

I was such a fantastically good credit risk that I already owned a Diners Club card. Zip! My signature on the dotted line and I was the proud possessor of two tickets (first class, no less) to the City of Lovers.

Jenny looked kind of pale and gray when I got home, but I hoped my fantastic idea would put some color in those cheeks.

'Guess what, Mrs Barrett,' I said.

'You got fired,' guessed my optimistic wife.

'No. Fired up,' I replied, and pulled out the tickets.

'Up, up and away,' I said. 'Tomorrow night to Paris.'

'Bullshit, Oliver,' she said. But quietly, with none of her usual mock-aggression. As she spoke it then, it was a kind of endearment: 'Bullshit, Oliver.'

'Hey, can you define "bullshit" more specifically, please?'

'Hey, Ollie,' she said softly, 'that's not the way we're gonna do it.'

'Do what?' I asked.

'I don't want Paris. I don't need Paris. I just want you—'

'That you've got, baby!' I interrupted, sounding falsely merry.

'And I want time,' she continued, 'which you can't give me.'

Now I looked into her eyes. They were ineffably sad. But sad in a way only I understood. They were saying she was sorry. That is, sorry for me.

We stood there silently holding one another. Please, if one of us cries, let both of us cry. But preferably neither of us.

And then Jenny explained how she had been feeling 'absolutely shitty' and gone back to Dr Sheppard, not for consultation, but confrontation: Tell me what's wrong with me, dammit. And he did.

I felt strangely guilty at not having been the one to break it to her. She sensed this, and made a calculatedly stupid remark.

'He's a Yalie, Ol.'

'Who is, Jen?'

'Ackerman. The hematologist. A total Yalie. College *and* Med School.'

'Oh,' I said, knowing that she was trying to inject some levity into the grim proceedings.

'Can he at least read and write?' I asked.

'That remains to be seen,' smiled Mrs

Oliver Barrett, Radcliffe '64, 'but I know he can talk. And I wanted to talk.'

'Okay, then, for the Yalie doctor,' I said.

'Okay,' she said.

XIX

Now at least I wasn't afraid to go home, I wasn't scared about 'acting normal'. We were once again sharing everything, even if it was the awful knowledge that our days together were every one of them numbered.

There were things we had to discuss, things not usually broached by twenty-four-year-old couples.

'I'm counting on you to be strong, you hockey jock,' she said.

'I will, I will,' I answered, wondering if the always knowing Jennifer could tell that the great hockey jock was frightened.

'I mean, for Phil,' she continued. 'It's gonna be hardest for him. You, after all, you'll be the merry widower.'

'I won't be merry,' I interrupted.

'You'll be merry, goddammit. I want you to be merry. Okay?'

'Okay.'

'Okay.'

It was about a month later, right after dinner. She was still doing the cooking; she insisted on it. I had finally persuaded her to allow me to clean up (though she gave me heat about it not being 'man's work'), and was putting away the dishes while she played Chopin on the piano. I heard her stop in mid-Prelude, and walked immediately into the living room. She was just sitting there.

'Are you okay, Jen?' I asked, meaning it in a relative sense. She answered with another question.

'Are you rich enough to pay for a taxi?' she asked.

'Sure,' I replied. 'Where do you want to go?'

'Like—the hospital,' she said.

I was aware, in the swift flurry of motions that followed, that this was it. Jenny was going to walk out of our apartment and never come back. As she just sat there while I threw a few things together for her, I wondered what was crossing her mind. About the apartment, I mean. What would she want to look at to remember?

Nothing. She just sat still, focusing on nothing at all.

'Hey,' I said, 'anything special you want to take along?'

'Uh uh.' She nodded no, then added as an after-thought, 'You.'

Downstairs it was tough to get a cab, it being theater hour and all. The doorman was blowing his whistle and waving his arms like a wild-eyed hockey referee. Jenny just leaned against me, and I secretly wished there would be no taxi, that she would just keep leaning on me. But we finally got one. And the cabbie was—just our luck—a jolly type. When he heard Mount Sinai Hospital on the double, he launched into a whole routine.

'Don't worry, children, you're in experienced hands. The stork and I have been doing business for years.'

In the back seat, Jenny was cuddled up against me. I was kissing her hair.

'Is this your first?' asked our jolly driver.

I guess Jenny could feel I was about to snap at the guy, and she whispered to me:

'Be nice, Oliver. He's trying to be nice to us.'

'Yes, sir,' I told him. 'It's the first, and my wife isn't feeling so great, so could we jump a few lights, please?'

He got us to Mount Sinai in nothing flat. He *was* very nice, getting out to open the door for us and everything. Before taking off again, he wished us all sorts of good fortune and happiness. Jenny thanked him.

She seemed unsteady on her feet and I wanted to carry her in, but she insisted, 'Not this threshold, Preppie.' So we walked in and suffered through that painfully nitpicking process of checking in.

'*Do you have Blue Shield or other medical plan?*'

'No.'

(Who could have thought of such trivia? We were too busy buying dishes.)

Of course, Jenny's arrival was not unexpected. It had earlier been foreseen and was now being supervised by Bernard Ackerman, M.D., who was, as Jenny predicted, a good guy, albeit a total Yalie.

'She's getting white cells and platelets,' Dr Ackerman told me. 'That's what she needs most at the moment. She doesn't want antimetabolites at all.'

'What does that mean?' I asked.

'It's a treatment that slows cell destruction,' he explained, 'but—as Jenny knows—there can be unpleasant side effects.'

'Listen, doctor'—I know I was lecturing him needlessly—'Jenny's the boss. Whatever she says goes. Just you guys do everything you possibly can to make it not hurt.'

'You can be sure of that,' he said.

'I don't care what it costs, doctor.' I think I was raising my voice.

'It could be weeks or months,' he said.

'Screw the cost,' I said. He was very patient with me. I mean, I was bullying him, really.

'I was simply saying,' Ackerman explained, 'that there's really no way of knowing how long—or how short—she'll linger.'

'Just remember, doctor,' I commanded him, 'just remember I want her to have the very best. Private room. Special nurses. Everything. Please. I've got the money.'

XX

It is impossible to drive from East Sixty-third Street, Manhattan, to Boston, Massachusetts, in less than three hours and twenty minutes. Believe me, I have tested the outer limits on this track, and I am certain that no automobile, foreign or domestic, even with some Graham Hill type at the wheel, can make it faster. I had the MG at a hundred and five on the Mass Turnpike.

I have this cordless electric razor and you can be sure I shaved carefully, and changed my shirt in the car, before entering those hallowed offices on State Street. Even at 8 A.M. there were several distinguished-looking Boston types waiting to see Oliver Barrett III. His secretary—who knew me—didn't blink twice when she spoke my name into the intercom.

My father did not say, 'Show him in.'

Instead, his door opened and he appeared in person. He said, 'Oliver.'

Preoccupied as I was with physical appearances, I noticed that he seemed a bit pale, that his hair had grown grayish (and perhaps thinner) in these three years.

'Come in, son,' he said. I couldn't read the tone. I just walked toward his office.

I sat in the 'client's chair'.

We looked at one another, then let our gazes drift onto other objects in the room.

I let mine fall among the items on his desk: scissors in a leather case, letter opener with a leather handle, a photo of Mother taken years ago. A photo of me (Exeter graduation).

'How've you been, son?' he asked.

'Well, sir,' I answered.

'And how's Jennifer?' he asked.

Instead of lying to him, I evaded the issue—although it *was* the issue—by blurting out the reason for my sudden reappearance.

'Father, I need to borrow five thousand dollars. For a good reason.'

He looked at me. And sort of nodded, I think.

'Well?' he said.

'Sir?' I asked.

'May I know the reason?' he asked.

'I can't tell you, Father. Just lend me the dough. Please.'

I had the feeling—if one can actually receive feelings from Oliver Barrett III—that he intended to give me the money. I also sensed that he didn't want to give me any heat. But he did want to . . . talk.

'Don't they pay you at Jonas and Marsh?' he asked.

'Yes, sir.'

I was tempted to tell him how much, merely to let him know it was a class record, but then I thought if he knew where I worked, he probably knew my salary as well.

'And doesn't she teach too?' he asked.

Well, he doesn't know everything.

'Don't call her "she",' I said.

'Doesn't Jennifer teach?' he asked politely.

'And please leave her out of this, Father. This is a personal matter. A very important personal matter.'

'Have you gotten some girl in trouble?'

he asked, but without any deprecation in his voice.

'Yeah,' I said, 'yes, sir. That's it. Give me the dough. Please.'

I don't think for a moment he believed my reason. I don't think he really wanted to know. He had questioned me merely, as I said before, so we could . . . talk.

He reached into his desk drawer and took out a checkbook bound in the same cordovan leather as the handle of his letter opener and the case for his scissors. He opened it slowly. Not to torture me, I don't think, but to stall for time. To find things to say. Non-abrasive things.

He finished writing the check, tore it from the book and then held it out toward me. I was maybe a split second slow in realizing I should reach out my hand to meet his. So he got embarrassed (I think), withdrew his hand and placed the check on the edge of his desk. He looked at me now and nodded. His expression seemed to say, 'There it is, son.' But all he really did was nod.

It's not that I wanted to leave, either. It's just that I myself couldn't think of anything neutral to say. And we couldn't just sit there, both of us willing to talk and yet unable even to look the other straight in the face.

I leaned over and picked up the check. Yes, it said five thousand dollars, signed Oliver Barrett III. It was already dry. I folded it carefully and put it into my shirt pocket as I rose and shuffled to the door. I should at least have said something to the effect that I knew that on my account very important Boston dignitaries (maybe even Washington) were cooling their heels in his outer office, and yet if we had more to say to one another I could even hang around your office, Father, and you would cancel your luncheon plans . . . and so forth.

I stood there with the door half open, and summoned the courage to look at him and say:

'Thank you, Father.'

XXI

The task of informing Phil Cavilleri fell to me. Who else? He did not go to pieces as I feared he might, but calmly closed the house in Cranston and came to live in our apartment. We all have our idiosyncratic ways of coping with grief. Phil's was to clean the place. To wash, to scrub, to polish. I don't really understand his thought processes, but Christ, let him work.

Does he cherish the dream that Jenny will come home?

He does, doesn't he? The poor bastard. That's why he's cleaning up. He just won't accept things for what they are. Of course, he won't admit this to me, but I know it's on his mind.

Because it's on mine too.

* * *

Once she was in the hospital, I called old man Jonas and let him know why I couldn't be coming to work. I pretended that I had to hurry off the phone because I know he was pained and wanted to say things he couldn't possibly express. From then on, the days were simply divided between visiting hours and everything else. And of course everything else was nothing. Eating without hunger, watching Phil clean the apartment (again!)

and not sleeping even with the prescription Ackerman gave me.

Once I overheard Phil mutter to himself, 'I can't stand it much longer.' He was in the next room, washing our dinner dishes (by hand). I didn't answer him, but I did think to myself, I can. Whoever's Up There running the show, Mr Supreme Being, sir, keep it up, I can take this ad infinitum. Because Jenny is Jenny.

That evening, she kicked me out of the room. She wanted to speak to her father 'man to man.'

'This meeting is restricted only to Americans of Italian descent,' she said, looking as white as her pillows, 'so beat it, Barrett.'

'Okay,' I said.

'But not too far,' she said when I reached the door.

I went to sit in the lounge. Presently Phil appeared.

'She says to get your ass in there,' he

whispered hoarsely, like the whole inside of him was hollow. 'I'm gonna buy some cigarettes.'

'Close the goddamn door,' she commanded as I entered the room. I obeyed, shut the door quietly, and as I went back to sit by her bed, I caught a fuller view of her. I mean, with the tubes going into her right arm, which she would keep under the covers. I always liked to sit very close and just look at her face, which, however pale, still had her eyes shining in it.

So I quickly sat very close.

'It doesn't hurt, Ollie, really,' she said. 'It's like falling off a cliff in slow motion, you know?'

Something stirred deep in my gut. Some shapeless thing that was going to fly into my throat and make me cry. But I wasn't going to. I never have. I'm a tough bastard, see? I am not gonna cry.

But if I'm not gonna cry, then I can't open my mouth. I'll simply have to nod yes. So I nodded yes.

'Bullshit,' she said.

'Huh?' It was more of a grunt than a word.

'You don't know about falling off cliffs, Preppie,' she said. 'You never fell off one in your goddamn life.'

'Yeah,' I said, recovering the power of speech. 'When I met you.'

'Yeah,' she said, and a smile crossed her face. '"Oh, what a falling off was there." Who said that?'

'I don't know,' I replied. 'Shakespeare.'

'Yeah, but who?' she said kind of plaintively. 'I can't remember which play, even. I went to Radcliffe, I should remember things. I once knew all the Mozart Köchel listings.'

'Big deal,' I said.

'You bet it was,' she said, and then screwed

up her forehead, asking, 'What number is the C Minor Piano Concerto?'

'I'll look it up,' I said.

I knew just where. Back in the apartment, on a shelf by the piano. I would look it up and tell her first thing tomorrow.

'I used to know,' Jenny said, 'I did. I used to know.'

'Listen,' I said, Bogart style, 'do you want to talk music?'

'Would you prefer talking funerals?' she asked.

'No,' I said, sorry for having interrupted her.

'I discussed it with Phil. Are you listening, Ollie?'

I had turned my face away.

'Yeah, I'm listening, Jenny.'

'I told him he could have a Catholic service, you'd say okay. Okay?'

'Okay,' I said.

'Okay,' she replied.

And then I felt slightly relieved, because after all, whatever we talked of now would have to be an improvement.

I was wrong.

'Listen, Oliver,' said Jenny, and it was in her angry voice, albeit soft. 'Oliver, you've got to stop being sick!'

'Me?'

'That guilty look on your face, Oliver, it's sick.'

Honestly, I tried to change my expression, but my facial muscles were frozen.

'It's nobody's fault, you preppie bastard,' she was saying. 'Would you please *stop* blaming yourself!'

I wanted to keep looking at her because I wanted to never take my eyes from her, but still I had to lower my eyes. I was so ashamed that even now Jenny was reading my mind so perfectly.

'Listen, that's the only goddamn thing I'm asking, Ollie. Otherwise, I know you'll be okay.'

That thing in my gut was stirring again, so I was afraid to even speak the word 'okay'. I just looked mutely at Jenny.

'Screw Paris,' she said suddenly.

'Huh?'

'Screw Paris and music and all that crap you think you stole from me. I don't care, you sonovabitch. Can't you believe that?'

'No,' I answered truthfully.

'Then get the hell out of here,' she said. 'I don't want you at my goddamn deathbed.'

She meant it. I could tell when Jenny really meant something. So I bought permission to stay by telling a lie:

'I believe you,' I said.

'That's better,' she said. 'Now would you do me a favor?' From somewhere inside me came this devastating assault to make me cry. But I withstood. I would *not* cry. I would merely indicate to Jennifer—by the affirmative nodding of my head—that I would be happy to do her any favor whatsoever.

'Would you please hold me very tight?' she asked.

I put my hand on her forearm—Christ, so thin—and gave it a little squeeze.

'No, Oliver,' she said, 'really hold me. Next to me.'

I was very, very careful—of the tubes and things—as I got onto the bed with her and put my arms around her.

'Thanks, Ollie.'

Those were her last words.

XXII

Phil Cavilleri was in the solarium, smoking his nth cigarette, when I appeared.

'Phil?' I said softly.

'Yeah?' He looked up and I think he already knew.

He obviously needed some kind of physical comforting. I walked over and placed my hand on his shoulder. I was afraid he might cry. I was pretty sure I wouldn't. Couldn't. I mean, I was past all that.

He put his hand on mine.

'I wish,' he muttered, 'I wished I hadn't ... .' He paused there, and I waited. What was the hurry, after all?

'I wish I hadn't promised Jenny to be strong for you.'

And, to honor his pledge, he patted my hand very gently.

But I had to be alone. To breathe air. To take a walk, maybe. Downstairs, the hospital lobby was absolutely still. All I could hear was the click of my own heels on the linoleum.

'Oliver.'

I stopped.

It was my father. Except for the woman at the reception desk we were all by ourselves there. In fact, we were among the few people in New York awake at that hour.

I couldn't face him. I went straight for the revolving door. But in an instant he was out there standing next to me.

'Oliver,' he said, 'you should have told me.'

It was very cold, which in a way was good because I was numb and wanted to feel *something*. My father continued to address me, and I continued to stand still and let the cold wind slap my face.

'As soon as I found out, I jumped into the car.'

I had forgotten my coat; the chill was starting to make me ache. Good. Good.

'Oliver,' said my father urgently, 'I want to help.'

'Jenny's dead,' I told him.

'I'm sorry,' he said in a stunned whisper.

Not knowing why, I repeated what I had long ago learned from the beautiful girl now dead.

'Love means not ever having to say you're sorry.'

And then I did what I had never done in his presence, much less in his arms. I cried.